Norman Robert Pogson, Madras Observatory

Telegraphic Determinations

of the difference of longitude between Karachi, Avanashi, Roorkee,

Pondicherry, Colombo, Jaffna, Muddapur and Singapore, and the

Government Observatory, Madras

Norman Robert Pogson, Madras Observatory

Telegraphic Determinations
of the difference of longitude between Karachi, Avanashi, Roorkee, Pondicherry, Colombo, Jaffna, Muddapur and Singapore, and the Government Observatory, Madras

ISBN/EAN: 9783337385743

Printed in Europe, USA, Canada, Australia, Japan

Cover: Foto ©Andreas Hilbeck / pixelio.de

More available books at **www.hansebooks.com**

TELEGRAPHIC DETERMINATIONS

DIFFERENCE OF LONGITUDE

BETWEEN

KARACHI, AVANASHI, ROORKEE, PONDICHERRY, COLOMBO, JAFFNA, MUDDAPUR AND SINGAPORE,

AND THE

GOVERNMENT OBSERVATORY, MADRAS,

BY

NORMAN R. POGSON, C.I.E.,

F.R.A.S. AND F.M.U.

Government Astronomer at Madras.

MADRAS:

PRINTED AT THE LAWRENCE ASYLUM PRESS, BY W. H. MOORE.

1884.

CONTENTS.

TELEGRAPHIC LONGITUDE DETERMINATIONS IN INDIA.

The telegraphic longitude determinations, details of which are now given in a collected form, were none of them taken under perfectly satisfactory conditions, such as were available to the officers of the Great Trigonometrical Survey in their far more elaborate series of measurements made a few years later.

The impossibility of interchanging observers or of settling their relative personal equations, and the want of proper chronographs, left in each case a small uncertainty, insignificant in comparison of the best values obtainable by any other method than that of telegraphic signals, but nevertheless existent and incapable of elimination from the results.

So long since as the end of 1861, I proposed to the Government of Madras an extensive series of telegraphic longitude measurements, and in the "Proceedings of the Madras Government, 11th January, 1862," I was called upon to report what arrangements would be required to carry out my views in determining the relative longitudes of Bombay, Beypore and Trevandrum on the West Coast, and of Calcutta, Cocanada and Negapatam on the East, from the Madras Observatory. In my report, submitted on the 30th of the same month, I pointed out the desirability of such determinations, the very moderate outlay involved, and the processes which then appeared to me most suitable for the purpose. On the 22nd September 1862, I submitted further specifications of the instruments required for the purpose, and was most desirous of doing what has since been so ably accomplished by the officers of the Great Trigonometrical Survey, but the matter was allowed to drop and my plans fell through in consequence.

The need of a good cylinder chronograph for other purposes, especially for investigation of the solar parallax by means of observations of the planet Mars in opposition, for which Madras Observatory is above all others the most favorably situated in the world, was often urged, but to this day nothing of the kind has been supplied, except a French tape recorder, sent out in November 1874, for the Transit of Venus due in the following month ;—a mere toy which no astronomer would care to possess and which has never been of the slightest use since its arrival. The chronographs now constructed by leading American and British makers are as near perfection as can be desired, and enable inexperienced observers to make records, equal, if not superior to those obtainable by long practised observatory assistants without such aid ; while in cases in which numerous times have to be noted, in more rapid succession than any one could possibly accomplish by the old eye and ear method, they are simply indispensable. American chronographs seem to me preferable for their greater simplicity, having only one pen or pencil for both clock seconds and observer's records, instead of two, separately marking side by side ; and also in their being worked by a portable chronometer, just as readily as by a fixed astronomical clock.

So far as the Madras portion of the eight following longitude determinations is concerned, the star observations for local time have been reduced, by application of the known personal equation for each transit observer, to my own standard ; but never having even seen the gentlemen with whom I had to co-operate in five cases, and having had no opportunity of comparing our habits of observation in any, except that of Avanashi, the small difference due to personal equation between myself and the operator at the other end remains in each case indeterminate. The probable errors for the mean results of transit observations and telegraphic signals on each night have been deduced by Professor C. H. F. Peters' convenient formula (disregarding algebraic signs and squaring) by multiplying each of the means of the Residual Errors by $\frac{0\cdot845}{\sqrt{n-1}}$; and these, combined in the usual way, show, for the final results for each place, the small amounts of uncertainty attributable to the time found by the star transits and to the exchanges of telegraphic signals, over and above which there will still remain the unknown personal equations and the errors of coincidence comparisons whenever a different time-piece was used for finding local time and for noting the signals. The latter cannot exceed two or three hundredths at the most, but the former may amount to a sensible fraction of a second. In no instance however is it likely that any result will be so much as a second of time in error, and for the purposes for which seven of these determinations were made, *viz.*, for the Total Solar Eclipse of December 1871 and the Venus Transit in December 1874, no such accuracy was required.

The longitude or difference of time between Madras and Greenwich was first approximately determined by Mr. John Goldingham, by means of eclipses of Jupiter's satellites, between 1787 and 1815, and was communicated by him to the Royal Society as $5h. 21m. 9·4s.$ Additional observations of the same nature, taken between 1817 and 1826, confirmed this result, giving a mean value only $0·4s.$ less but about 10 seconds too great as now determined.

The next astronomer, Mr T. G. Taylor, realizing the now familiar fact, that time found by eclipses of Jupiter's satellites is extremely uncertain, differing with the telescopic aperture and power employed, as well as with the conditions of the atmosphere, twilight, moonlight, and most of all perhaps with the observer's health and visual perception, had recourse to the far better method of moon culminators, and from a few observations in 1831 obtained a smaller value, *viz.*, $5h. 21m. 3·77s.$ which was adopted in the Nautical Almanac list from 1835 to 1861. A much closer approximation was, subsequently, arrived at by Mr. Taylor from the discussion of lunar observations between 1831 and 1844, which gave $5h. 20m. 57·2s.$; but though published in 1845 it was overlooked and not admitted into the Nautical Almanac list until 1862.

The adopted value $5h. 20m. 59·4s.$ given in the Nautical Almanac since 1882, is a combination result, in which the telegraphic longitude of Suez, by members of the Transit of Venus Expedition in 1874, was combined with others, between Suez, Aden, Bombay and Madras, made by the officers of the Great Trigonometrical Survey of India in 1876 and 1877.

Should a final trial by means of direct signals between the Greenwich and Madras Transit Clocks ever be accomplished, verification rather than correction will probably be all that can be expected from the undertaking.

PONDICHERRY.

The first telegraphic determination of the difference of longitude between Madras and any other station in India was made conjointly by myself at Madras and by Mons. G. Fleuriais at Pondicherry. The reasons for this undertaking are best given in M. Fleuriais' own words, in the following letter addressed to me by that able and distinguished officer.

PONDICHERRY, 5th Decembre 1869.

MONSIEUR LE DIRECTEUR,

En Avril 1867, J'ái été chargé par le bureau des longitudes de France, d'une Mission Scientifique ayant pour objet la recherche, par la methode astronomique dite *des Culminations lunaires*, des longitudes *absoluès* d'un certain nombre de points du globe.

Mes instructions m'enjoignaient ;

1°, d'observer à Paris, pendant 3 mois au moins, avec les instruments que j'emporterais en voyage, afin de m'habituer au maniement de ces derniers et de determiner trés exactement mon équation personnelle.

2°, D'accomplir un tour du monde complet en sejournant sur les Points suivants : Montévideo, Sandy Point (de N. de Magellan), Valparaiso, Callao, Panama, Honolulu, Yokohama, Shanghai, Pondicherry.

3°, De revenir à Paris et d'y déterminer de nouveau la valeur de mon équation personnelle.

Sur les 9 stations désignées, 8 sont achevées. Arrivé à Pondicherry le 27 Novembre, je termine actuellement le montage d'une Lunette méridienne qui me permettra de commencer, dès la réapparition de la Lune, les observations qui m'incombent.

Comme vous l'avez, dejá compris, le but que se propose le Bureau des Longitudes est l'obtention d'un certain nombre de *Méridiens fondamentaux* qui poussaient ultériéurement servir à la verification des points intermediaires.

Partout où je l'ai pu, J'ai cherché à relier les villes environnants au point où je sejournai moi-même, soit au moyen du télégraphe electrique, soit par traversée chronometriques.

Les résultats que je vais m'efforcer d'obtenir ici, n'auront qu'un bien médiocre interet s'ils ne s'adressent qu'à Pondicherry.

Il n'en serait point de même si cette dernière ville pouvait etre reliée aux grands Centres des Indes.

Les différences des méridiens de Bombay, Calcutta, Madras ont, je crois déjá été obtenues au moyen du télégraphe. Mais aucune opération de ce genre n'a encore en lieu sur Pondicherry.

Votre présence à Madras, jointe à l'existence d'une ligne télégraphique directe (où pouvant etre etablie en communication directe) entre ce point et Pondicherry, m'a fait penser que vous vous occupeiz avec plaisir de la détermination des différences d'heures des deux villes en question. ·

Une semblable opération, si j'en juge par l'analogue que j'ai du faire en 1868 entre Santiago et Valparaiso, ne demanderait guére que *le like usage* du télégraphe pendant 2 heures au plus ; mais auparavant, il faudrait etablir, par correspondance, des conventions simples et nettes, faire quelques démarches officielles, enfin convenir d'un jour et d'une heure donnée pour laquelle il serait facile à vous et a moi d'obtenir le reglage parfait de un ou plusieurs chronometres.

Dans cette circonstance tout depend de votre volonté. Je n'ai donc voulu ni parler de ce projet á Monsieur le Gouverneur ni entrer dans aucun detail d'execution. J'attends pour cela votre réponse, qui, si elle est favorable comme je l'espere, exciterait un vif sentiment de reconnaissance chez ceux dont je ne suis que le mandataire. ·

Veuillez agréer Monsieur le directeur, &c., &c.

(Signed) G. FLEURIAIS,

Lieutenant de Vaisseau, en Mission Scientifique á Pondicherry (gouvernement.)

It is needless to state that the opportunity thus afforded me of co-operating with Monsieur Fleuriais was most willingly complied with, and the few requisite preliminary preparations being made, the work was successfully carried out on January 14th, 1870. The use of the telegraph wire was readily granted us by the Government Telegraph Department, and the local officers in charge rendered us the most cordial aid at each end of the line. My thanks were especially due on this occasion to G. Barclay, Esq., Assistant Superintendent at Madras.

The local sidereal time at Madras being found by ten good transit observations, a mean time chronometer was compared with the transit clock by means of coincident beats and was then carefully transported to the Government Telegraph Office about three miles distant, where the signals, consisting of sharp taps on the Morse instrument employed for the usual telegraphic messages, were both given and recorded by me personally, in preference to noting those sent by a signaller, a precaution which no doubt renders the results far more certain than when the latter course is adopted. The mean time chronometer was then taken back to the Observatory and again compared with the Transit clock, its rate being determined solely from the comparisons made before and after the operations.

At Pondicherry precisely the same course was followed by Mons. Fleuriais, his local sidereal time being also found by ten clock stars, using a sidereal chronometer by Bréguet, and for comparison and signalling a mean time one by Leroy. The time determinations, comparisons and signals are given in the following tables, but it is to be regretted that Mons. Fleuriais only sent me five out of the thirty-eight signals transmitted to him, viz., the first and last of each set, and one intermediate one which he considered preferable to all others as being an absolute coincidence. No retardation, either of current or instruments, was perceptible on this occasion.

In publishing telegraphic longitude determinations it is usual to suppress the individual signals and to give only mean results, but I have exhibited all in detail, so as to render the admission of a single erroneous step impossible throughout.

The special geographical points referred to in this determination are, the centres of the Transit Circle in the Madras Observatory and of the Lighthouse at Pondicherry. The difference of time between Mons. Fleuriais' temporary observatory and the Light-house was given by him 0·56 second, as obtained by triangulation with a theodolite.

MADRAS. || PONDICHERRY.

Local Sidereal Time Determinations, 1870, January 14.

Name of Star.	Transit Clock.		Sidereal Correction.	Residual Errors.	Name of Star.	Chronometer Bréguet, 889.		Sidereal Correction.		Residual Errors.
	h.	m.	s.	s.		h.	m.	m.	s.	s.
δ Arietis	3	5	− 34·22	+ 0·01	α Ceti.........	2	57	− 1	15·13	+ 0·11
Alcyone	3	40	− 34·32	− 0·06	δ Arietis ...	3	5	− 1	15·24	0·00
o′ Eridani.....	4	6	− 34·36	− 0·08	Alcyone......	3	41	− 1	15·27	− 0·01
ε Tauri.........	4	22	− 34·33	− 0·04	γ′ Eridani ...	3	55	− 1	15·31	− 0·04
Aldebaran.....	4	29	− 34·28	+ 0·01	ε Can. Maj...	6	55	− 1	15·28	+ 0·08
γ Geminorum.	6	31	− 34·30	+ 0·08	η Can. Maj...	6	59	− 1	15·34	+ 0·02
ε Can. Maj....	6	54	− 34·37	+ 0·03	δ Geminorum	7	14	− 1	15·31	+ 0·05
δ Geminorum	7	13	− 34·29	+ 0·12	ζ Can. Min...	7	21	− 1	15·39	− 0·02
Procyon........	7	33	− 34·43	. 0·00	Castor........	7	28	− 1	15·42	− 0·05
Pollux.........	7	38	− 34·45	− 0·02	Procyon......	7	34	− 1	15·47	− 0·10
Means	5	33	− 34·34	0·045	Means	5	43	− 1	15·32	0·048
Adopted daily change.................... − 1·07					Adopted daily change... .... − 0·70					

NOTE.—The adopted daily change duly allowed for in finding the Residual Errors.

Comparisons of Chronometers used for Signalling.

Transit Clock.	Sidereal Correction.	Chronometer Dent 1668.	Mean Time Correction.	Chronometer Bréguet 889.	Sidereal Correction.	Chronometer Leroy 227.	Mean Time Correction.
h. m. s.	s.	h. m. s.	s.	h. m. s.	m. s.	h. m. s.	m. s.
4 26 0	− 34·29	8 57 54·0	− 10·54	5 53 50	− 1 15·31	10 20 13·5	− 1 35·53
8 6 12	− 34·45	12 37 29·5	− 10·28	7 57 10	− 1 15·38	12 29 13·5	− 1 35·81

Madras and Pondicherry Time Corrections, 1870, *January* 14.

At 8*h.* 58*m.* by Mr. Pogson's Chronometer Dent 1868, it was 10·54 seconds fast of Madras Mean Time with an adopted daily rate of 1·70 seconds losing.

At 10*h.* 26*m.* by M. Fleuriais' Chronometer Leroy 227, it was 1*m.* 35·53*s.* fast of Pondicherry Mean Time, with an adopted daily rate of 3·27 seconds gaining.

Hence at 10 *h.* 25*m.* by Chronometer Dent 1668, the relative correction was 1*m.* 25·09*s.*, and its change + 0·00345 second per minute.

Telegraphic Signals from Madras to Pondicherry.

Madras Signals.	Pondicherry Records.	Difference. Mad.—Pon.	Relative Correction.	Pondicherry West.	Residual Errors.
h. m. s.	*h. m. s.*	*s.*	*m. s.*	*m. s.*	*s.*
10 0 30	10 0 15·75	14·25	1 25·01	1 39·26	− 0·01
10 0	9 45·75	14·25	1 25·04	1 39·29	+ 0·02
11 30	11 15·80	14·20	1 25·04	1 39·24	− 0·03
18 30	18 15·80	14·20	1 25·07	1 39·27	0·00
10 20 0	10 19 45·80	14·20	1 25·07	1 39·27	0·00
10 12 6·00	10 11 51·78	14·22	1 25·05	1 39·27	0·012

Telegraphic Signals from Pondicherry to Madras.

Madras Records.	Pondicherry Signals.	Difference Mad.—Pon.	Relative Correction.	Pondicherry West.	Residual Errors.
h. m. s.	*h. m. s.*	*s.*	*m. s.*	*m. s.*	*s.*
10 30 29·3	10 30 15	14·3	1 25·11	1 39·41	+ 0·14
30 44·2	30 30	14·2	1 25·11	1 39·31	+ 0·04
31 14·2	31 0	14·2	1 25·11	1 39·31	+ 0·04
31 29·3	31 15	14·3	1 25·11	1 39·41	+ 0·14
10 31 44·3	10 31 30	14·3	1 25·11	1 39·41	+ 0·14

Telegraphic Signals from Pondicherry to Madras.

Madras. Records.			Pondicherry Signals.			Difference Mad.—Pon.	Relative Correction.		Pondicherry West.		Residual Errors.
h.	*m.*	*s.*	*h.*	*m.*	*s.*	*s.*	*m.*	*s.*	*m.*	*s.*	*s.*
10	32	14·2	10	32	0	14·2	1	25·11	1	39·31	+ 0·04
	32	29·2		32	15	14·2	1	25·12	1	39·32	+ 0·05
	32	44·1		32	30	14·1	1	25·12	1	39·22	− 0·05
	33	14·2		33	0	14·2	1	25·12	1	39·32	+ 0·05
	33	29·2		33	15	14·2	1	25·12	1	39·32	+ 0·05
	33	44·2		33	30	14·2	1	25·12	1	39·32	+ 0·05
	34	14·1		34	0	14·1	1	25·12	1	39·22	− 0·05
	34	29·2		34	15	14·2	1	25·12	1	39·32	+ 0·05
	34	44·3		34	30	14·3	1	25·12	1	39·42	+ 0·15
	35	14·2		35	0	14·2	1	25·13	1	39·33	+ 0·00
	35	29·0		35	15	14·0	1	25·13	1	39·13	− 0·14
	35	44·2		35	30	14·2	1	25·13	1	39·33	+ 0·00
	36	14·1		36	0	14·1	1	25·13	1	39·23	− 0·04
	36	44·2		36	30	14·2	1	25·13	1	39·33	+ 0·06
	37	14·1		37	0	14·1	1	25·13	1	39·23	− 0·04
	37	29·2		37	15	14·2	1	25·13	1	39·33	+ 0·06
	37	44·2		37	30	14·2	1	25·13	1	39·33	+ 0·06
	38	14·0		38	0	14·0	1	25·14	1	39·14	− 0·13
	38	44·1		38	30	14·1	1	25·14	1	39·24	− 0·03
	39	14·2		39	0	14·2	1	25·14	1	39·34	+ 0·07
	39	29·1		39	15	14·1	1	25·14	1	39·24	− 0·03
	39	44·1		39	30	14·1	1	25·14	1	39·24	− 0·03
	41	29·1		41	15	14·1	1	25·15	1	39·25	− 0·02
	41	44·0		41	30	14·0	1	25·15	1	39·15	− 0·12
	42	14·2		42	0	14·2	1	25·15	1	39·35	+ 0·08
	42	29·0		42	15	14·0	1	25·15	1	39·15	− 0·12
	42	44·2		42	30	14·2	1	25·15	1	39·35	+ 0·08
	43	14·1		43	0	14·1	1	25·15	1	39·25	− 0·02
	43	29·0		43	15	14·0	1	25·15	1	39·15	− 0·12
	43	44·1		43	30	14·1	1	25·15	1	39·25	− 0·02
	44	14·1		44	0	14·1	1	25·16	1	39·26	− 0·01
	44	29·2		44	15	14·2	1	25·16	1	39·36	+ 0·09
	44	44·0		44	30	14·0	1	25·16	1	39·16	− 0·11
	45	14·0		45	0	14·0	1	25·16	1	39·16	− 0·11
	45	44·0		45	30	14·0	1	25·16	1	39·16	− 0·11
	46	14·2		46	0	14·2	1	25·16	1	39·36	+ 0·09
	46	29·0		46	15	14·0	1	25·16	1	39·16	− 0·11
	46	44·3		46	30	14·3	1	25·16	1	39·46	+ 0·19
	47	14·0		47	0	14·0	1	25·17	1	39·17	− 0·10
10	47	29·1	10	47	15	14·1	1	25·17	1	39·27	0·00

3

Telegraphic Signals from Pondicherry to Madras.

Madras Records.			Pondicherry Signals.			Difference Mad.—Pon.	Relative Correction.		Pondicherry West.		Residual Errors.
h.	*m.*	*s.*	*h.*	*m.*	*s.*	*s.*	*m.*	*s.*	*m.*	*s.*	*s.*
10	47	44·0	10	47	30	14·0	1	25·17	1	39·17	− 0·10
	48	14·1		48	0	14·1	1	25·17	1	39·27	0·00
	48	29·0		48	15	14·0	1	25·17	1	39·17	− 0·10
	48	44·2		48	30	14·2	1	25·17	1	39·37	+ 0·10
	49	14·0		49	0	14·0	1	25·17	1	39·17	− 0·10
	49	29·0		49	15	14·0	1	25·17	1	39·17	− 0·10
	49	44·0		49	30	14·0	1	25·18	1	39·18	− 0·09
	50	14·0		50	0	14·0	1	25·18	1	39·18	− 0·09
	50	29·1		50	15	14·1	1	25·18	1	39·23	+ 0·01
10	50	44·2	10	50	30	14·2	1	25·18	1	39·38	+ 0·11
10	40	40·68	10	40	26·45	14·13	1	25·14	1	39·27	0·075

Hence by five signals to and fifty-five from Pondicherry, Monsieur Fleuriais[f] temporary Observatory was 1*m.* 39·27*s.* West of Madras.

Final Results.

	h.	*m.*	*s.*
Madras Observatory East of Greenwich ...	5	20	59·40
Pondicherry Observing Station West of Madras.	−	1	39·27
Pondicherry Light-house East of Observing Station		+	0·56
Pondicherry Light-house East of Greenwich ...	5	19	20·69
Probable Error of result, exclusive of Personal Equation		±	0·020

SINGAPORE.

The second application for a telegraphic longitude determination was made to me by Professor J. A. C. Oudemans, Surveyor General of Java, in November, 1870, and was one of the greatest interest, from its importance as a link in the telegraphic line from Greenwich to Australia. Professor Oudemans had already connected Batavia, the capital of Dutch India, with Singapore, and the cable between the latter place and Madras having been very recently laid, he hoped to have been granted its use early in 1871. The permission came too late, and Professor Oudemans had to return to Batavia without carrying out his plans. The cordial offers of co-operation on the part of the officials of the British India Extension Telegraph Company, without which success would have been improbable, induced him to make a further representation of the importance of the work to his Government ; and this meeting with favorable consideration, I had great pleasure in lending willing aid to the scheme. Telegraphic correspondence, most freely and liberally granted by the Company, enabled us speedily to arrange all details, and the work was accomplished on the four nights, July 24th, 25th, 26th and 28th, 1871.

Owing to unfortunate interruptions and other causes it is to be regretted that no steps towards the calculation of the results were possible until January, 1876, when I first received Professor Oudemans' time corrections and records of signals. The individual clock corrections not having been furnished me, I can only express my hope and belief, that Professor Oudemans has modestly underrated the accuracy of his observations for time and I cannot acquiesce in the rejection of any one of the four results obtained. In his abstract, published in the "*Astronomisches Nachrichten No. 2486*" he has used only the mean of the signals exchanged on the first and third nights, whereas, if I had rejected any, it would have been those of the third night, in consequence of a too large change in the correction of the mean time chronometer I used for giving and noting the signals. The work on the last night was, on my side, probably the best of the four, and in any case I consider none so doubtful as to be unworthy of acceptance.

There is a small difference between my clock corrections now given and those furnished to Professor Oudemans, arising from change in the adopted personal equations of my assistants, which were then only provisionally assumed, but have since been finally settled, so far as can be done, from all the observations made for the purpose. Altogether, my final longitude of

Singapore is 0·25 second more than Professor Oudemans deduced, and 0·54 less than has since been found by Lieut. Commander C. H. Davis and Lieut. J. A. Morris of the U. S. Navy, in January, 1882. The exquisite instruments I had the pleasure of seeing employed here by my esteemed American friends Messrs. Davis and Lemley, as well as the skilful way in which they were handled, were the realization of what I had hoped for when I first made my own proposals to Government for longitude determinations upon my arrival in India. Perfection of accurate simplicity, eschewing all affectation of needless refinement, seems to be the distinguishing characteristic of American scientific instruments and researches in general, and of such nature were the appliances and methods used upon this occasion.

The operations for determining the difference of longitude between Madras and Singapore require little explanation beyond what is given in the following tabular statements. · The points referred to were, the Madras Transit Circle and the Singapore Government Flagstaff. As in the case of Pondicherry, a mean time chronometer was compared with the Madras Transit Clock and conveyed to and from the Office of the British Indian Extension Telegraph Company, about four miles from the Observatory. An unsatisfactory change in the chronometer rate, in the interval between the before and after comparisons, occurred on July 26th, but the result does not appear to have been much affected thereby. At Singapore, Professor Oudemans used a mean time chronometer for the signals on the first night, but on the other three the sidereal chronometer with which his transits were observed. The signal taps were given at each end by ourselves, but the records are far more difficult by cable than on a land line ; the lateral motion of a small flash of light, reflected from a tiny mirror on a screen, appearing to an observer far less satisfactory than the sharp tap of a Morse instrument.

The scheme agreed upon was, twelve signals at fifteen seconds interval from Madras ; the same from Singapore, and both operations repeated ; but I see no advantage in such interrupted records and prefer to treat all sent the same way as one series each night. One or two signals were occasionally missed, but each result was so similar in quality, that weights on that account were unnecessary.

The Mean Retardation, which is of course due partly to actual wave retardation through the cable and partly to inertia in the instruments at each end, called by the American observers " Wave and armature time," was smaller in our case than in theirs, arising no doubt from the use of a greater battery power in 1871 than in 1882.

Local Sidereal and Mean Time Determinations.

	MADRAS.			SINGAPORE.
Star.	Transit Clock.	Sidereal Correction.	Residual. Errors.	All Time Corrections reduced to the position of the Government Flagstaff.
	1871, July 24.			1871, July 24.
	h. m.	s.	s.	
Antares	16 21	+ 58·44	0·00	
ζ Herculis	16 35	+ 58·55	+ 0·11	Time determinations made by means of an excellent Universal Instrument by Repsold, and a Mean Time Chronometer, Schmidt 325.
κ Ophiuchi....	16 · 51	+ 58·38	− 0·06	
α Herculis	17 8	+ 58·51	+ 0·08	Two zenith distances of Arcturus observed in one position and one in another. Also four zenith distances each of Altair and β Ceti.
θ Ophiuchi....	17 13	+ 58·35	− 0·08	
α Ophiuchi....	17 28	+ 58·39	− 0·03	
μ Herculis	17 40	+ 58·46	+ 0·04	
μ¹ Sagittarii.	18 5	+ 58·30	− 0·11	
ζ Aquilæ......	18 59	+ 58·38	− 0·02	
δ Aquilæ......	19 18	+ 58·39	0·00	
λ² Sagittarii.	19 28	+ 58·32	− 0·07	
Altair..........	19 44	+ 58·52	+ 0·14	
β Aquilæ......	19 48	+ 58·41	+ 0·03 ·	
α² Capricorni	20 10	+ 58·37	0·00	

Star.	Chronometer.	Correction.
	h. m.	m. s.
Arcturus	8 8	−2 21·065
Altair....................	13 40	−2 20·47
β Ceti....................	14 5	−2 20·67
Adopted daily change ...	...	... + 2·07

	MADRAS.		
Means..........	18 12	+ 58·41	0·055
Probable error of mean correction ...			± 0·013
Adopted daily change			− 0·45

	1871, July 25.			1871, July 25.
λ² Sagittarii.	19 28	+ 58·17	+ 0·23	
γ Aquilæ......	19 39	+ 57·89	− 0·04	Sidereal Time found with a new portable Transit Instrument by Wenckebach, the eyepiece of which was at one extremity of the axis. The Chronometer used was Hohwn 394. No details of the observations communicated, but the estimated uncertainty of the result given as 0·15 second.
Altair..........	19 44	+ 57·97	+ 0·04	
β Aquilæ......	19 48 ·	+ 57·91	− 0·02	
ρ Capricorni..	20 21	+ 57·81	− 0·11	
32 Vulpeculæ.	20 48	+ 57·60	− 0·11	

	MADRAS.			SINGAPORE.
Star.	Transit Clock.	Sidereal Correction.	Residual Errors.	All Time Corrections reduced to the position of the Government Flagstaff.

	1871, July 25—*continued.*			1871, July 25—*continued.*
	h. m.	*s.*	*s.*	
ζ Cygni........	21 7	+ 57·94	+ 0·03	
β Aquarii......	21 24	+ 57·87	− 0·03	*h. m.* *s.*
ε Pogasi........	. 21 37	+ 57·89	− 0·01	At 17 30 the correction was ....+ 24·56
				Adopted daily change ....+ 2·33
Means	20 26	+ 57·92	0·069	

Probable error of mean correction ...   ± 0·021

Adopted daily change ...   .   − 0·42

	1871, July 26.			1871, July 26.
κ Ophiuchi....	16 51	+ 57·55	− 0·03	
α Herculis.....	17 8	+ 57·62	+ 0·04	Sidereal Time found with the portable Transit
α Ophiuchi....	17 28	+ 57·56	− 0·01	Instrument and Chronometer Hohwn 394, as
μ Herculis.....	17 40	+ 57·67	+ 0·10	follows :—
μ Sagittarii ...	18 5	+ 57·55	− 0·01	*s.*
ζ Aquilæ......	18 59	+ 57·51	− 0·04	By six stars eyepiece East + 28·085
μ Aquilæ......	19 11	+ 57·49	− 0·06	By five stars eyepiece West + 28·238
δ Aquilæ......	19 18	+ 57·60	+ 0·05	By six stars eyepiece East + 28·259
γ Aquilæ......	19 39	+ 57·48	− 0·06	*h. m.* *s.*
Altair..........	19 44	+ 57·58	+ 0·04	Hence at 18 0 the correction was..... + 27·04
				Its estimated uncertainty................ 0·10
Means	18 24	+ 57·56	0·044	Adopted daily change .... + 2·28

Probable error of mean correction   ±0·012

Adopted daily change   − 0·36

MADRAS.				SINGAPORE.
Star.	Transit Clook.	Sidereal Corrections.	Residual Errors.	All Time Corrections reduced to the position of the Government Flagstaff.
	1871, July 28.			1871, July 28.
	h. m.	s.	s.	
« Herculis....	17 40	+ 56·73	− 0·06	Sidereal Time found with the portable Transit Instrument and Chronometer Hohwn 394 as
Vega............	18 32	+ 56·80	+ 0·03	follows:—
ζ Aquilœ......	18 59	+ 56·72	− 0·05	
ω Aquilœ......	19 11	+ 56·77	+ 0·01	s.
				By five stars eyepiece East + 33·904
δ Aquilœ......	19 18	+ 56·70	− 0·06	By ten stars eyepiece West + 33·514
γ Aquilœ......	19 39	+ 56·79	+ 0·04	By seven stars eyepiece East + 33·318
Altair.........	19 44	+ 56·83	+ 0·08	h. m. s.
β Aquilæ......	19 48	+ 56·74	− 0·01	At 22 40 the correction was........,.. +32·40
α² Capricorni	20 10	+ 56·77	+ 0·02	Its estimated uncertainty.................... 0·20
ρ Capricorni..	20 21	+ 56·73	− 0·01	Adopted daily change............................ + 2·88
Means.........	19 20	+ 56·76	0·037	
Probable error of mean correction			±0·010	
Adopted daily change			−0·40	

Comparisons of Madras Chronometer used for Signalling.

Transit Clook.	Sidereal Correction.	Chronometer Dent 1668.	Mean Time Correction.	Transit Clock.	Sidereal Correction.	Chronometer Dent 1668.	Mean Time Correction.
1871, July 24.				1871, July 26.			
h. m. s.	s.	h. m. s.	s.	h. m. s.	s.	h. m. s.	s.
17 45 2	+ 58·42	9 38 16	− 2·20	17 46 1	+ 57·57	9 31 14	+ 5·97
20 24 2	+ 58·37	12 16 50	− 2·30	19 46 6	+ 57·54	11 31 0	+ 5·27
1871, July 25.				1871, July 28.			
17 55 28	+ 57·96	9 44 40	+ 1·72	18 12 37	+ 56·78	9 49 45	+ 14·01
20 25 3	+ 57·92	12 13 50	+ 2·17	20 54 0	+ 56·73	12 30 41	+ 14·52

Madras and Singapore Time Corrections, 1871, *July* 24.

At 9 *h.* 38 *m.* by Mr. Pogson's Chronometer Dent 1668, it was 2·20 seconds fast of Madras Mean Time, with an adopted daily rate of 0·91 second gaining.

At 13 *h.* 52·5 *m.* by Prof. Oudeman's. Chronometer Schmidt 325, it was 2 *m.* 20·57 *s.* fast of Singapore Mean Time, with an adopted daily rate of 2·07 seconds losing.

Hence at 11 *h.* 13 *m.* by Chronometer Dent 1668, the relative correction was 2 *m.* 18·40 *s.* and its change — 0·00207 second per minute.

Telegraphic Signals from Madras to Singapore.

Madras Signals.			Singapore Records.			Difference Sing.—Mad.			Relative Correction.		Singapore East.			Residual Errors.
h.	m..	s.	h.	m.	s.	h.	m.	s.	m.	s.	h.	m.	s.	s.
10	45	0	12	21	42·50	1	36	42·50	2	18·46	1	34	24·04	+ 0·01
	45	15		21	57·35		36	42·35	2	18·46		34	23·89	− 0·14
	45	30		22	12·50		36	42·50	2	18·46		34	24·04	+ 0·01
	45	45		22	27·50		36	42·50	2	18·46		34	24·04	+ 0·01
	46	0		22	42·45		36	42·45	2	18·46		34	23·99	− 0·04
	46	15		22	57·50		36	42·50	2	18·46		34	24·04	+ 0·01
	46	30		23	12·40		36	42·40	2	18·45		34	23·95	− 0·08
	46	45		23	27·45		36	42·45	2	18·45		34	24·00	− 0·03
	47	0		23	42·50		36	42·50	2	18·45		34	24·05	+ 0·02
	47	15		23	57·50		36	42·50	2	18·45		34	24·05	+ 0·02
	47	30		24	12·45		36	42·45	2	18·45		34	24·00	− 0·03
	57	30		34	12·50		36	42·50	2	18·43		34	24·07	+ 0·04
	57	45		34	27·45		36	42·45	2	18·43		34	24·02	− 0·01
	58	0		34	42·50		36	42·50	2	18·43		34	24·07	+ 0·04
	58	15		34·	57·50	·	36	42·50	2	18·43		34	24·07	+ 0·04
	58	45		35	27·50		36	42·50	2	18·43		34	24·07	+ 0·04
	59	0		35	42·50		36	42·50	2	18·43		34	24·07	+ 0·04
	59	15		35	57·50		36	42·50	2	18·43		34	24·07	+ 0·04
	59	30		36	12·40		36	42·40	2	18·43		34	23·97	− 0·06
	59	45		36	27·50		36	42·50	2	18·43		34	24·07	+ 0·04
11	0	0	12	36	42·50	1	36	42·50	2	18·43		34	24·07	+ 0·04
11	52	12·86	12	28	55·33	1	36	42·47	· 2	18·44	1	34	24·03	0·038

Telegraphic Signals from Singapore to Madras, 1871, July 24.

Madras Records.			Singapore Signals.			Difference. Sing.—Mad.			Relative Correction.		Singapore East.			Residual Errors.
h.	m.	s.	h.	m.	s.	h.	m.	s.	m.	s.	h.	m.	s.	s.
10	50	34.0	12	27	15.50	1	36	41.50	2	18.45	1	34	23.05	+0.16
	50	49.0		27	30.35		36	41.35	2	18.45		34	22.90	+0.01
	51	4.4		27	45.60		36	41.20	2	18.45		34	22.75	-0.14
	51	33.9		28	15.05		36	41.15	2	18.44		34	22.71	-0.18
	51	48.5		28	30.10		36	41.60	2	18.44		34	23.16	+0.27
	52	4.0		28	45.25		36	41.25	2	18.44		34	22.81	-0.06
	52	19.0		29	0.30		36	41.30	2	18.44		34	22.86	-0.03
	52	34.0		29	15.40		36	41.40	2	18.44		34	22.96	+0.07
	52	48.6		29	30.00		36	41.40	2	18.44		34	22.96	+0.07
	53	4.0		29	45.30		36	41.30	2	18.44		34	22.86	-0.03
	53	19.0		30	0.25		36	41.25	2	18.44		34	22.81	-0.08
11	1	34.0		38	14.95		36	40.95	2	18.42		34	22.53	-0.36
	1	48.9		38	30.20		36	41.30	2	18.42		34	22.88	-0.01
	2	4.0		38	45.25		36	41.25	2	18.42		34	22.83	-0.06
	2	16.8		39	0.40		36	41.60	2	18.42		34	23.18	+0.29
	2	33.6		39	15.00		36	41.40	2	18.42		34	22.98	+0.09
	2	48.5		39	29.95		36	41.45	2	18.42		34	23.03	+0.14
	3	4.0		39	45.50		36	41.50	2	18.42		34	23.08	+0.19
	3	19.0		40	0.30		36	41.30	2	18.42		34	22.88	-0.01
	3	33.8		40	15.05		36	41.25	2	18.42		34	22.83	-0.06
	3	49.0		40	30.25		36	41.25	2	18.42		34	22.83	-0.06
	4	4.0		40	45.25		36	41.25	2	18.42		34	22.83	-0.06
11	4	19.0	12	41	0.25	1	36	41.25	2	18.42	1	34	22.83	-0.06
10	57	42.39	12	34	23.71	1	36	41.32	2	18.43	1	34	22.89	0.100

Madras and Singapore Time Corrections, 1871, July 25.

At 9h. 45m. by Mr. Pogson's Chronometer Dent 1668, it was 1·72 seconds slow of Madras Mean Time, with an adopted daily rate of 4·34 seconds losing.

At 17h. 30m. by Prof. Oudeman's Sidereal Chronometer Hohwn 394, it was 24·56 seconds slow of Singapore Sidereal Time, with an adopted daily rate of 2·33 seconds losing.

Hence at 10h. 45m. by Chronometer Dent 1668, the relative correction was 8h. 11m. 31·20s. and its change + 0·16567 second per minute.

Telegraphic Signals from Madras to Singapore, 1871, July 25.

Madras Signals.			Singapore Records.			Difference. Sing.—Mad.			Relative Correction.			Singapore East.			Residual Errors.
h.	m.	s.	h.	m.	s.	h.	m.	s.	h.	m.	s.	h.	m.	s.	s.
10	35	15	20	21	8·50	9	45	53·50	8	11	29·58	1	34	23·92	− 0·11
	35	30		21	23·65		45	53·65		11	29·63		34	24·02	− 0·01
	35	45		21	38·80		45	53·80		11	29·67		34	24·13	+ 0·10
	36	0		21	53·80		45	53·80		11	29·71		34	24·09	+ 0·06
	36	15		22	8·60		45	53·60		11	29·75		34	24·05	+ 0·02
	36	30		22	23·90		45	53·90		11	29·79		34	24·11	+ 0·08
	36	45		22	39·00		45	54·00		11	29·83		34	24·17	+ 0·14
	37	0		22	54·00		45	54·00		11	29·87		34	24·13	+ 0·10
	37	15		23	9·00		45	54·00		11	29·91		34	24·09	+ 0·06
	37	30		23	24·00		45	54·00		11	29·96		34	24·04	+ 0·01
	37	45		23	39·00		45	54·00		11	30·00		34	24·00	− 0·03
	38	0		23	54·00		45	54·00		11	30·04		34	23·96	− 0·07
	49	15		35	11·00		45	56·00		11	31·90		34	24·10	+ 0·07
	49	30		35	26·00		45	56·00		11	31·94		34	24·06	+ 0·03
	49	45		35	41·00		45	56·00		11	31·99		34	24·01	− 0·02
	50	0		35	56·05		45	56·05		11	32·03		34	24·02	− 0·01
	50	15		36	11·10		45	56·10		11	32·07		34	24·03	0·00
	50	30		36	26·10		45	56·10		11	32·11		34	23·99	− 0·04
	50	45		36	41·05		45	56·05		11	32·15		34	23·90	− 0·13
	51	0		36	56·10		45	56·10		11	32·19		34	23·91	− 0·12
	51	15		37	11·15		45	56·15		11	32·23		34	23·92	− 0·11
	51	30		37	26·25		45	56·25		11	32·27		34	23·98	− 0·05
	51	45		37	41·25		45	56·25		11	32·32		34	23·93	− 0·10
10	52	0	20	37	56·45	9	45	56·45	8	11	32·36	1	34	24·09	+ 0·06
10	43	37·50	20	29	32·50	9	45	55·00	8	11	30·97	1	34	24·03	0·064

Telegraphic Signals from Singapore to Madras, 1871, July 25.

Madras Records.			Singapore Signals.			Difference. Sing.—Mad.			Relative Correction.			Singapore East.			Residual Errors.
h.	m.	s.	h.	m.	s.	h.	m.	s.	h.	m.	s.	h.	m.	s.	s.
10	44	21·0	20	30	15	9	45	54·0	8	11	31·09	1	34	22·91	+ 0·04
	44	36·0		30	30		45	54·0		11	31·13		34	22·87	0·00
	44	50·9		30	45		45	54·1		11	31·17		34	22·93	+ 0·06
	45	6·0		31	0		45	54·0		11	31·22		34	22·78	− 0·09
	45	20·9		31	15		45	54·1		11	31·26		34	22·84	− 0·03
	45	36·0		31	30		45	54·0		11	31·30		34	22·70	− 0·17
	45	50·8		31	45		45	54·2		11	31·34		34	22·86	− 0·01
	46	5·9		32	0		45	54·1		11	31·38		34	22·72	− 0·15
	46	20·5		32	15		45	54·5		11	31·42		34	23·08	+ 0·21
	46	35·5		32	30		45	54·5		11	31·46		34	23·04	+ 0·17
	46	50·6		32	45		45	54·4		11	31·50		34	22·90	+ 0·03
	47	5·5		33	0		45	54·5		11	31·54		34	22·96	+ 0·09
	53	34·5		39	30		45	55·5		11	32·62		34	22·88	+ 0·01
	53	49·4		39	45		45	55·6		11	32·66		34	22·94	+ 0·07
	54	4·5		40	0		45	55·5		11	32·70		34	22·80	− 0·07
	54	19·5		40	15		45	55·5		11	32·74		34	22·76	− 0·11
	54	34·5		40	30		45	55·5		11	32·79		34	22·72	− 0·15
	54	49·5		40	45		45	55·5		11	32·83		34	22·67	− 0·20
	55	4·4		41	0		45	55·6		11	32·87		34	22·73	− 0·14
	55	19·2		41	15		45	55·8		11	32·91		34	22·89	+ 0·02
	55	34·1		41	30		45	55·9		11	32·95		34	22·95	+ 0·08
	55	49·0		41	45		45	56·0		11	32·99		34	23·01	+ 0·14
	56	4·0		42	0		45	56·0		11	33·03		34	22·97	+ 0·10
10	56	19·0	20	42	15	9	45	56·0	8	11	33·07	1	34	22·93	+ 0·06
10	50	20·05	20	36	15·00	9	45	54·95	8	11	32·08	1	34	22·87	0·092

Madras and Singapore Time Corrections, 1871, *July* 26.

At 9*h*. 31*m*. by Mr. Pogson's Chronometer Dent 1668, it was 5·97 seconds slow of Madras Mean Time, with an adopted daily rate of 8·42 seconds gaining.

At 18*h*. 0*m*. by Prof. Oudeman's Chronometer Hohwn 394, it was 27·04 seconds slow of Singapore Sidereal Time, with an adopted daily rate of 2·28 seconds losing.

Hence at 10*h*. 25*m*. by Chronometer Dent 1668, the relative correction was 8*h*. 15*m*. 25·83*s*. and its change + 0·15685 second per minute.

Telegraphic Signals from Madras to Singapore, 1871, *July* 26.

Madras Signals.			Singapore Records.			Difference. Sing.—Mad.			Relative Correction.			Singapore East.			Residual Errors.
h.	*m.*	*s.*	*h.*	*m.*	*s.*	*h.*	*m.*	*s.*	*h.*	*m.*	*s.*	*h.*	*m.*	*s.*	*s.*
10	16	30	20	6	18·55	9	49	48·55	3	15	24·49	1	34	24·06	0·00
	16	45		6	33·60		49	48·60		15	24·53		34	24·07	+ 0·01
	17	0		6	48·60		49	48·60		15	24·57		34	24·03	− 0·03
	17	15		7	3·70		49	48·70		15	24·61		34	24·09	+ 0·03
	17	30		7	18·65		49	48·65		15	24·65		34	24·00	− 0·06
	17	45		7	33·75		49	48·75		15	24·69		34	24·06	0·00
	18	0		7	48·65		49	48·65		15	24·73		34	23·92	− 0·14
	18	15		8	3·75		49	48·75		15	24·77		34	23·98	− 0·08
	18	30		8	18·80		49	48·80		15	24·81		34	23·99	− 0·07
	18	45		8	33·95		49	48·95		15	24·85		34	24·10	+ 0·04
	19	0		8	49·00		49	49·00		15	24·80		34	24·11	+ 0·05
	31	15		21	6·00		49	51·00		15	26·81		34	24·19	+ 0·13
	31	30		21	21·00		49	51·00		15	26·85		34	24·15	+ 0·09
	31	45		21	36·00		49	51·00		15	26·89		34	24·11	+ 0·05
	32	0		21	51·05		49	51·05		15	26·93		34	24·12	+ 0·06
	32	15		22	6·15		49	51·15		15	26·97		34	24·18	+ 0·12
	32	30		22	21·05		49	51·05		15	27·01		34	24·04	− 0·02
	32	45		22	36·05		49	51·05		15	27·05		34	24·00	− 0·06
	33	0		22	51·15		49	51·15		15	27·08		34	24·07	+ 0·01
	33	15		23	6·10		49	51·10		15	27·12		34	23·98	− 0·08
	33	30		23	21·25		49	51·25		15	27·16		34	24·09	+ 0·03
	33	45		23	36·20		49	51·20		15	27·20		34	24·00	− 0·06
10	34	0	20	23	51·20	9	49	51·20	8	15	27·24	1	34	23·96	− 0·10
10	25	30·65	20	15	20·62	9	49	49·97	8	15	25·91	1	34	24·06	0·057

Telegraphic Signals from Singapore to Madras, 1871, July 26.

Madras Records.			Singapore Signals.			Difference. Sing.—Mad.			Relative Correction.			Singapore East.			Residual Errors.
h.	*m.*	*s.*	*h.*	*m.*	*s.*	*h.*	*m,*	*s.*	*h.*	*m.*	*s.*	*h,*	*m.*	*s.*	*s.*
10	20	42·1	20	10	30	9	49	47·9	8	15	25·16	1	34	22·74	− 0·24
	20	56·9		10	45		49	48·1		15	25·19		34	22·91	− 0·07
	21	12·0		11	0		49	48·0		15	25·23		34	22·77	− 0·21
	21	26·8		11	15		49	48·2		15	25·27		34	22·93	− 0·05
	21	41·9		11	30		49	48·1		15	25·31		34	22·79	− 0·19
	21	56·6		11	45		49	48·4		15	25·35		34	23·05	+ 0·07
	22	11·5		12	0		49	48·5		15	25·39		34	23·11	+ 0·13
	22	26·5		12	15		49	48·5		15	25·43		34	23·07	+ 0·09
	22	41·6		12	30		49	48·4		15	25·47		34	22·93	− 0·05
	22	56·5		12	45		49	48·5		15	25·81		34	22·99	+ 0·01
	23	11·5		13	0		49	48·5		15	25·55		34	22·95	− 0·03
	23	26·5		13	15		49	48·5		15	25·59		34	22·91	− 0·07
	35	24·5		25	15		49	50·5		15	27·46		34	23·04	+ 0·06
	35	39·5		25	30		49	50·5		15	27·50		34	23·00	+ 0·02
	35	54·5		25	45		49	50·5		15	27·54		34	22·96	− 0·02
	36	9·5		26	0		49	50·5		15	27·58		34	22·92	− 0·06
	36	24·4		26	15		49	50·6		15	27·62		34	22·98	0·00
	36	39·4		26	30		49	50·6		15	27·66		34	22·94	− 0·04
	36	54·3		26	45		49	50·7		15	27·70		34	23·00	+ 0·02
	37	9·2		27	0		49	50·8		15	27·74		34	23·06	+ 0·08
	37	24·0		27	15		49	51·0		15	27·78		34	23·22	+ 0·24
	37	39·1		27	30		49	50·9		15	27·81		34	23·09	+ 0·11
	37	54·0		27	45		49	51·0		15	27·85		34	23·15	+ 0·17
10	38	9·1	20	28	0	9	49	50·9	8	15	27·89	1	34	23·01	+ 0·03
10	29	25·50	20	19	15·00	9	49	49·50	8	15	26·52	1	34	22·98	0·086

Madras and Singapore Time Corrections, 1871, *July* 28.

At 9*h*. 50*m*. by Mr. Pogson's Chronometer Dent 1668, it was 14·01 seconds slow of Madras Mean Time, with an adopted daily rate of 4·56 seconds losing.

At 22*h*. 40*m*. by Professor Oudeman's Chronometer Hohwn 394, it was 32·40 seconds slow of Singapore Sidereal Time, with an adopted daily rate of 2·88 seconds losing.

Hence at 10*h*. 33*m*. by Chronometer Dent 1668, the relative correction was 8*h*. 23*m*. 23·88*s*. and its change + 0·16545 seconds per minute. .

Telegraphic Signals from Madras to Singapore, 1871, *July* 28.

Madras Signals.			Singapore Records.			Difference. Sing.—Mad.			Relative Correction.			Singapore East.			Residual Errors.
h.	m.	s.	h.	m.	s.	h.	m.	s.	h.	m.	s.	h.	m.	s.	s.
10	30	15	20	28	2·85	9	57	47·85	8	23	23·43	1	34	24·42	+ 0·05
	30	30		28	17·95		57	47·95		23	23·47		34	24·48	+ 0·11
	30	45		28	32·95		57	47·95		23	23·51		34	24·44	+ 0·07
	31	0		28	47·90		57	47·90		23	23·55		34	24·35	− 0·02
	31	15		29	3·00		57	48·00		23	23·59		34	24·41	+ 0·04
	31	30		29	18·00		57	48·00		23	23·63		34	24·37	0·00
	31	45		29	33·00		57	48·00		23	23·67		34	24·33	− 0·04
	32	0		29	48·05		57	48·05		23	23·71		34	24·34	− 0·03
	32	15		30	3·10		57	48·10		23	23·76		34	24·34	− 0·03
	32	30		30	18·10		57	48·10		23	23·80		34	24·30	− 0·07
	32	45		30	33·05		57	48·05		23	23·84		34	24·21	− 0·16
	33	0		30	48·25		57	48·25		23	23·88		34	24·37	0·00
	39	15		37	4·50		57	49·50		23	24·91		34	24·59	+ 0·22
	39	30		37	19·35		57	49·35		23	24·96		34	24·39	+ 0·02
	39	45		37	34·35		57	49·35		23	25·00		34	24·35	− 0·02
	40	0		37	49·40		57	49·40		23	25·04		34	24·36	− 0·01
	40	15		38	4·50		57	49·50		23	25·08		34	24·42	+ 0·05
	40	30		38	19·50		57	49·50		23	25·12		34	24·38	+ 0·01
	40	45		38	34·50		57	49·50		23	25·16		34	24·34	− 0·03
	41	0		38	49·55		57	49·55		23	25·20		34	24·35	− 0·02
	41	15		39	4·55		57	49·55		23	25·25		34	24·30	− 0·07
10	41	30	20	39	19·60	9	57	49·60	8	23	25·29	1	34	24·31	− 0·06
10	35	36·14	20	33	24·82	9	57	48·68	8	23	24·31	1	34	24·37	0·051

Telegraphic Signals from Singapore to Madras, 1871, July 28.

Madras Records.			Singapore Signals.			Difference. Sing.—Mad.			Relative Correction.			Singapore East.			Residual Errors.
h.	m.	s.	h.	m.	s.	h.	m.	s.	h.	m.	s.	h.	m.	s.	s.
10	34	12·6	20	32	0	9	57	47·4	8	23	24·08	1	34	23·32	+ 0·03
	34	27·5		32	15		57	47·5		23	24·12		34	23·38	+ 0·09
	34	42·4		32	30		57	47·6		23	24·16		34	23·44	+ 0·15
	34	57·5		32	45		57	47·5		23	24·20		34	23·30	+ 0·01
	35	12·5		33	0		57	47·5		23	24·24		34	23·26	− 0·03
	35	27·5		33	15		57	47·5		23	24·29		34	23·21	− 0·06
	35	42·4		33	30		57	47·6		23	24·33		34	23·27	− 0·02
	35	57·5		33	45		57	47·5		23	24·37		34	23·13	− 0·16
	36	12·3		34	0		57	47·7		23	24·41		34	23·29	0·00
	36	27·4		34	15		57	47·6		23	24·45		34	23·15	− 0·14
	36	42·1		34	30		57	47·9		23	24·49		34	23·41	+ 0·12
	36	57·0		34	45		57	48·0		23	24·53		34	23·47	+ 0·18
	43	11·2		41	0		57	48·8		23	25·57		34	23·23	− 0·06
	43	26·0		41	15		57	49·0		23	25·61		34	23·39	+ 0·10
	43	41·0		41	30		57	49·0		23	25·65		34	23·35	+ 0·06
	43	56·0		41	45		57	49·0		23	25·60		33	23·31	+ 0·02
	44	11·0		42	0		57	49·0		23	25·73		34	23·27	− 0·02
	44	26·0		42	15		57	49·0		23	25·77		34	23·23	− 0·06
	44	40·9		42	30		57	49·1		23	25·81		34	23·29	0·00
	44	55·9		42	45		57	49·1		23	25·85		34	23·25	− 0·04
	45	10·8		43	0		57	49·2		23	25·89		34	23·31	+ 0·02
	45	26·0		43	15		57	49·0		23	25·94		34	23·06	− 0·23
	45	40·8		43	30		57	49·2		23	25·98		34	23·22	− 0·07
10	45	55·6	20	43	45	0	57	49·4	8	23	26·02	1	34	23·38	+ 0·09
10	40	4·16	20	37	52·50	9	57	48·34	8	23	25·05	1	34	23·29	0·074

Summary of Telegraphic Results.

1871.	Number of Signals.		Singapore East.			Probable Errors.	Compound Retardation.
			h.	m.	s.	s.	s.
July 24 ...	By 21 from Madras	...	1	34	24·03	±·0·007	0·575
,, ,, ...	By 23 from Singapore	...	1	34	22·88	± 0·019	
,, 25 ...	By 24 from Madras	...	1	34	24·03	± 0·011	0·580
,, ,, ...	By 24 from Singapore	...	1	34	22·87	± 0·016	
,, 26 ...	By 23 from Madras	...	1	34	24·06	± 0·010	0·540
,, ,, ...	By 24 from Singapore	...	1	34	22·98	± 0·015	
,, 28 ...	By 22 from Madras	...	1	34	24·37	± 0·009	0·540
,, ,, ...	By 24 from Singapore	... ...	1	34	23·29	± 0·013	s.

Final Results.

	h.	m.	s.
Madras Observatory East of Greenwich	5	20	59·40
Singapore East of Madras...........................	1	34	23·56
Singapore East of Greenwich.........................	6	55	22·96
Probable Error of Signals and Madras Transits......			± 0·014
Compound Retardation (Current and Instruments).			0·549

AVANASHI.

A Government expedition being sanctioned for the observations of the Total Eclipse of the Sun which swept across Southern India on 1871, December 12th, the Railway Station nearest to the central line of totality naturally suggested itself as most convenient for the transport of a staff of observers, instruments, tents and all camp requisites, and with the kind permission of Mr. R. B. Elwin, Agent and Manager of the Madras Railway Company, the grounds of the Avanashi Station, in Coimbatore District, were selected for the purpose. Mr. G. K. Winter, the Company's Telegraph Engineer, who so ably assisted me upon a similar occasion at Masulipatam, in August, 1868, having again undertaken the polarisation observations of the Solar Corona, I was further favored with the use of the line to make a telegraphic longitude comparison with the Madras Observatory.

The point of reference at Avanashi was a small brick column, northeast of the Railway Station, built to hold the portable transit instrument brought from Madras. The transit instrument itself, an old one by Dollond, repaired but not improved, was very unsatisfactory in its level adjustment. Only four clock stars were observed either at Madras or at Avanashi on the night of the longitude operations, but the relative personal equations of the operators being known considerably within the limits of fluctuation to which such individual peculiarities or habits are liable, the longitude of Avanashi is probably more definitely settled than that of any other place in the determination of which I have participated.

My chief native assistant, the late C. Ragoonatha Charry, having only just returned to Madras, the signals were exchanged between him, at the Royaporam terminus of the line, about five miles from the Observatory, and myself at Avanashi. The noisy interruption of a train, arriving just as the records were commenced, led me to ask for more signals from Madras, but, as shown by the residual errors, really without cause. At each station a mean time chronometer was compared with the sidereal clock or chronometer by which the transits were observed, and was then carefully carried to the telegraph office as on previous occasions.

Local Sidereal Time Determinations, 1870, *December* 14.

MADRAS.				AVANASHI.			
Name of Star.	Transit Clock.	Sidereal Correction.	Residual Errors.	Name of Star.	Chronometer Hatton and Harris.	Sidereal Correction.	Residual Errors.
	h. m.	s.	s.		h. m.	s.	s.
θ Ceti.............	1 16	− 23·35	+ 0·06	61 Tauri.......	4 16	− 12·24	− 0·35
β Arietis... ..	1 48	− 23·54	− 0·11	Aldebaran...	4 29	− 11·52	+ 0·37
α Persei.......	3 16	− 23·46	+ 0·03	δ Orionis......	5 26	− 11·98	− 0·11
Alcyone.......	3 40	− 23·50	+ 0·01	ε Orionis......	5 30	− 11·80	+ 0·07
Means	2 30	− 23·46	0·053	Means.........	4 55	− 11·88	0·225

Probable Error of Mean Correction......... ± 0·026   Probable Error of mean correction .... ± 0·110

Adopted daily change.............................. − 1·00   Adopted daily change .... + 0·34

Comparisons of Chronometers used for Signalling.

Transit Clock.	Sidereal Correction.	Chronometer Arnold and Dent 1337.	Mean Time Correction.	Chronometer Hatton and Harris.	Sidereal Correction.	Chronometer Dent. 1668.	Mean Time Correction.
1870, December 14.				1870, December 13.			
h. m. s.	s.	h. m. s.	s.	h. m. s.	s.	h. m. s.	m. s.
1 6 9	− 23·40	7 34 30	+ 1·97	2 45 35	− 12·25	9 28 40	− 10 53·20
4 3 49	− 23·53	10 31 40	+ 2·73	1870, December 14.			
				8 1 44	− 11·84	14 40 1	− 10 52·60

Madras and Avanashi Time Corrections, 1871, December 14.

At 16 *h*. 32 *m*. by C. Ragoonatha Chary's Chronometer, Arnold and Dent 1337, it was 2·73 seconds slow of Madras Mean Time, with an adopted daily rate of 6·16 seconds losing.

At 14 *h*. 40 *m*. by Mr. Pogson's Chronometer, Dent 1668, it was 10 *m*. 52·60 *s*. fast of Avanashi Mean Time, with an adopted daily rate of 0·49 second losing.

Hence at 9 *h*. 15 *m*. by Arnold and Dent 1337, the relative correction was 10 *m*. 55·11 *s*. and its change + 0·00394 second per minute.

Telegraphic Signals from Madras to Avanashi, 1871, December 14.

Madras Signals.			Avanashi Records.			Difference. Mad.—Avan.	Relative Correction.		Avanashi West.		Residual Errors.
h.	*m*.	*s*.	*h*.	*m*.	*s*.	*s*.	*m*.	*s*.	*m*.	*s*.	*s*.
8	51	15	8	50	31·0	44·0	10	55·02	11	39·02	0·00
	51	30		50	46·0	44·0	10	55·02	11	39·02	0·00
	51	45		51	1·2	43·8	10	55·02	11	38·82	− 0·20
	52	0		51	16·0	44·0	10	55·02	11	39·02	0·00
	52	15		51	31·1	43·9	10	55·02	11	38·92	− 0·10
	52	30		51	46·0	44·0	10	55·02	11	39·02	0·00
	52	45		52	1·0	44·0	10	55·02	11	39·02	0·00
	53	0		52	16·2	43·8	10	55·02	11	38·82	− 0·2·0
	53	15		52	31·0	44·0	10	55·02	11	39·02	0·00
	53	30		52	46·0	44·0	10	55·03	11	39·03	+ 0·01
	53	45		53	1·0	44·0	10	55·03	11	39·03	+ 0·01
	54	0		53	16·2	43·8	10	55·03	11	38·83	− 0·19
	54	15		53	31·0	44·0	10	55·03	11	39·03	+ 0·01
	54	30		53	46·1	43·9	10	55·03	11	38·93	− 0·09
	55	0		54	16·0	44·0	10	55·03	11	39·03	+ 0·01
	55	15		54	31·0	44·0	10	55·03	11	39·03	+ 0·01
	55	45		55	1·0	44·0	10	55·03	11	39·03	+ 0·01
	56	0		55	16·0	44·0	10	55·04	11	39·04	+ 0·02
	56	15		55	31·0	44·0	10	55·04	11	39·04	+ 0·02
	56	30		55	46·0	44·0	10	55·04	11	39·04	+ 0·02
	56	45		56	1·0	44·0	10	55·04	11	39·04	+ 0·02
	57	0		56	16·0	44·0	10	55·04	11	39·04	+ 0·02
	57	15		56	31·0	44·0	10	55·04	11	39·04	+ 0·02
	58	30		57	46·0	44·0	10	55·04	11	39·04	+ 0·02
8	58	45	8	58	1·0	44·0	10	55·05	11	39·05	+ 0·03

Telegraphic Signals from Madras to Avanashi, 1871, December, 14.

Madras Signals.			Avanashi Records.			Difference. Mad.—Avan.	Relative Correction.		Avanashi East.		Residual Errors.
h.	m.	s.	h.	m.	s.	s.	m.	s.	m.	s.	s.
8	59	0	8	58	16·0	44·0	10	55·05	11	39·05	+ 0·03
	59	15		58	31·0	44·0	10	55·05	11	39·05	+ 0·03
	59	30		58	46·0	44·0	10	55·05	11	39·05	+ 0·03
	59	45		59	1·0	44·0	10	55·05	11	39·05	+ 0·03
9	0	0		59	16·1	43·9	10	55·05	11	38·95	+ 0·07
	0	15		59	30·9	44·1	10	55·05	11	39·15	+ 0·13
	0	30		59	46·0	44·0	10	55·05	11	39·C5	+ 0·03
	0	45	9	0	1·0	44·0	10	55·05	11	39·05	+ 0·03
	1	0		0	16·0	44·0	10	55·05	11	39·05	+ 0·03
	1	15		0	31·2	43·8	10	55·06	11	38·86	− 0·16
	1	30		0	46·0	44·0	10	55·06	11	39·06	+ 0·04
	1	45		1	1·0	44·0	10	55·06	11	39·06	+ 0·04
	2	0		1	16·0	44·0	10	55·06	11	39·06	+ 0·04
	2	15		1	31·0	44·0	10	55 06	11	39·06	+ 0·04
	2	30		1	46·0	44·0	10	55·06	11	39·06	+ 0·04
	2	45		2	1·0	44·0	10	55·06	11	39·06	+ 0·04
	3	0		2	16·0	44·0	10	55·06	11	39·06	+ 0·04
	3	15		2	31·0	44·0	10	55·06	11	39·06	+ 0·04
	3	30		2	46·0	44·0	10	55·06	11	39·06	+ 0·04
	3	45		3	1·1	43·9	10	55·07	11	38·97	− 0·05
	20	15		19	31·2	43·8	10	55·13	11	38·93	− 0·09
	20	30		19	46·1	43·9	10	55·13	11	39·03	+ 0·01
	20	45		20	1·0	44·0	10	55·13	11	39·13	+ 0·11
	21	0		20	16·2	43·8	10	55·13	11	38·93	− 0·09
	21	15		20	31·2	43·8	10	55·13	11	38·93	− 0·09
	21	30		20	46·0	44·0	10	55·14	11	39·14	+ 0·12
	21	45		21	1·3	43·7	10	55·14	11	38·84	− 0·18
	22	0		21	16·1	43·9	10	55·14	11	39·04	+ 0·02
	22	15		21	31·3	43·7	10	55·14	11	38·84	− 0·18
	22	30		21	46·1	43·9	10	55·14	11	39·04	+ 0·02
	22	45		22	1·0	44·0	10	55·14	11	39·14	+ 0·12
	23	0		22	16·1	43·9	10	55·14	11	39·04	+ 0·02
	23	15		22	31·1	43·9	10	55·14	11	39·04	+ 0·02
	23	30		22	46·1	43·9	10	55·14	11	39·04	+ 0·02
9	23	45	9	23	1·0	44·0	10	55·14	11	39·14	+ 0·12
9	3	40·75	9	2	56·80	43·95	10	55·07	11	39·02	0·053

Telegraphic Signals from Avanashi to Madras, 1871, December 14.

Madras Records.			Avanashi Signals.			Difference. Mad.—Avan.	Relative Correction.		Avanashi West.		Residual Errors.
h.	m.	s.	h.	m.	s.	s.	m.	s.	m.	s.	s.
9	10	59·1	9	10	15	44·1	10	55·09	11	39·19	+ 0·10
	11	14·0		10	30	44·0	10	55·10	11	39·10	+ 0·01
	11	28·0		10	45	43·9	10	55·10	11	39·00	− 0·09
	11	43·9		11	0	43·9	10	55·10	11	39·00	− 0·09
	11	59·0		11	15	44·0	10	55·10	11	39·10	+ 0·01
	12	14·0		11	30	44·0	10	55·10	11	39·10	+ 0·01
	12	28·8		11	45	43·8	10	55·10	11	38·90	− 0·19
	12	43·8		12	0	43·8	10	55·10	·11	38·90	· − 0·19
	12	58·9		12	15	43·9	10	55·10	11	39·00	− 0·09
	13	14·0		12	30	44·0	10.	55·10	11	39·10	+ 0·01
	13	29·0		12	45	44·0	10	55·10	11	39·10	+ 0·01
	13	44·0		13	0	44·0	10	55·11	11	39·11	+ 0·02
	13	59·1		13	15	44·1	10	55·11	11	39·21	+ 0·12
	14	14·0		13	30	44·0	10	55·11	11	39·11	+ 0·02
	14	29·0		13	45	44·0	10	55·11	11	39·11	+ 0·02
	14	44·1		14	0	44·1	10	55·11	11	39·21	+ 0·12
	14	59·0		14	15	44·0	10	55·11	11	39·11	+ 0·02
	15	14·0		14	30	44·0	10	55·11	11	39·11	+ 0·02
	15	29·1		14	45	44·1	10	55·11	11	39·21	+ 0·12
9	15	44·0	9	15	0	44·0	10	55·11	11	39·11	+ 0·02
9	13	21·49	9	12	37·50	43·99	10	55·10	11	39·09	0·064

						m.	s.	s.
Avanashi West by 60 Signals from Madras	...	...	...	...	11	39·02	± 0·006
Avanashi West by 20 Signals to Madras	...	...	...	...	11	39·09	± 0·012

Final Results.

		h.	m.	s.
Madras Observatory East of Greenwich.	...	5	20	59·40
Avanashi Transit Pillar West of Madras.	...		11	39·05
Avanashi Transit Pillar East of Greenwich.	...	5	9	20·35
Probable Error of Signals and Transits.	...		±	0·114
Retardation. (Current and Instruments.)	...			0·035

JAFFNA.

Longitude determinations of Jaffna and Colombo, in Ceylon, were requested by Captain (now Lieut-Colonel) J. L. Tupman, R. M. A., in connection with his observations of the total eclipse of the Sun, on 1871, December 11th. The Madras Observatory expedition to Avanashi for the same purpose prevented any exchanges of signals before the eclipse, but C. Ragoonathachary, the first native assistant, having been sent back immediately after, to aid in the Avanashi longitude determination, and Captain Tupman being desirous of leaving Jaffna as soon as possible, the first exchange was carried out on December 15th, before my return to Madras. The second, on December 16th was between Captain Tupman and myself.

On both these occasions the comparison and transport of a mean time chronometer was for the first time dispensed with, thanks to the obliging arrangements of P. V. Luke, Esq., the Officer in charge at the Madras Government Telegraph Office, who made temporary connections with the line from the Observatory used for firing the Fort Time Signal Gun ; thereby enabling the signals to be given and recorded from the transit clock direct, instead of as before, by the intervention of a chronometer.

The geographical point of reference at Jaffna was a stone pier, erected on purpose near the centre of the open parade ground within the Fort. The observations for local time were double altitudes of the Sun, taken by Captain Tupman, with an excellent three vernier reflecting circle by Messrs. Troughton and Simms, and a mercurial artificial horizon. The time-piece used was a very good marine chronometer, Muston, No. 610, beating half-seconds and shewing a few minutes short of Greenwich mean time. The probable errors of Captain Tupman's time determinations could not well be shewn, as the altitude observations were reduced in groups instead of singly ; but from the quality of the instruments employed and the evident care and skill of the observer, they must have been very small and would have made but a trifling increase in the probable error of the final result.

It is to be regretted that Captain Tupman's detailed records did not reach me until 1876, January 30th, and still more that a further and yet longer interval elapsed before I could again give the subject due attention. The subsequently far better established longitude of the Madras Observatory and the final deduction of the personal equations of each of my assistants enable me however, now to furnish final values, entitled to far more reliance than earlier reductions would have yielded.

Madras Sidereal Time Determinations.

Name of Star.	Transit Clock.	Sidereal Correction.	Residual Errors.	Name of Star.	Transit Clock.	Sidereal Correction.	Residual Errors.
	1871, December 15.				1871, December 16.		
	h. m.	s.	s.		h. m.	s.	s
ι Piscium	23 34	− 24·37	− 0·02	ι Piscium......	23 34	− 25·30	− 0·04
δ Sculptoris...	23 43	− 24·33	+ 0·02	δ Sculptoris ..	23 43	− 25·33	− 0·07
ω Piscium. ...	23 53	− 24·34	+ 0·02	ω Piscium	23 53	− 25·27	0·00
α Andromedæ	0 2	− 24·40	− 0·04	α Andromedæ	0 2	− 25·40	− 0·13
γ Pegasi.......	0 7	− 24·36	+ 0·01	γ Pegasi.......	0 7	− 25·27	+ 0·01
12 Ceti.........	0 24	− 24·40	− 0·02	12 Ceti	0 24	− 25·36	− 0·07
β Ceti..........	0 38	− 24·37	+ 0·02	β Ceti	0 38	− 25·28	+ 0·01
β Arietis......	1 48	− 24·49	− 0·06	γ¹ Eridani....	3 52	− 25·42	0·00
Aldebaran....	4 29	− 24·51	+ 0·03	ο Eridani	4 6	− 25·41	+ 0·02
Rigel	5 9	− 24·50	+ 0·07	ε Tauri.........	4 22	− 25·20	+ 0·24
Means	1 11	− 24·41	0·031	Mean........	1 16	− 25·32	0·059

Probable error of mean correction....... ± 0·010

Adopted daily change........................... − 0·96

Probable error of mean correction......... ± 0·020

Adopted daily change......................... − 0·92

Jaffna Mean Time Determinations.

1871, December 13.

By five double altitudes of the Sun's ·upper limb, followed by five more of the lower limb ; taken with a reflecting circle by Troughton & Simms, in reversed positions of both circle and artificial horizon, between 8 and 9 A.M. of December 14th, civil reckoning ;—the Chronometer, Muston 610, was 5h. 13m. 12·14s. slow, when it shewed 15h. 24m. ; corresponding to 20h. 38m. of Jaffna Mean Time, on December 13th.

1871 December, 15, 16.

By ten double altitudes of the Sun's upper limb and ten of the lower limb, taken with the same instruments and precautions as before, between 8 and 9 A.M. of December 16th, civil reckoning, combined with twenty more similar observations between 3 and 4 P.M., the Chronometer was 5h. 13m. 12·61s. slow, when it shewed 18h. 54m. ; corresponding to 0h. 8m. of Jaffna Mean Time, on December 16th. Its adopted daily rate was 0·22 second losing.

Madras and Jaffna Time Corrections, 1871, December 15.

At 1h. 11m. by the Madras Transit Clock, it was 24·41 seconds fast of Sidereal Time, with an adopted daily rate of 0·96 second gaining.

At 3h. 24m. by Captain Tupman's Chronometer, Muston 610, it was 5h. 13m. 12·47s. slow of Jaffna Mean Time, with an adopted daily rate of 0·22 second losing.

Hence at 2h. 19m. by the Madras Transit Clock, the relative correction was 1h. 11m. 1·59s. and its change − 0·16465 second per minute.

Telegraphic Signals from Madras to Jaffna, 1871, December 15.

Madras Signals.			Jaffna Records.			Difference. Jaff.—Mad.			Relative Correction.			Jaffna West.	Residual Errors.
h.	m.	s.	h.	m.	s.	h.	m.	s.	h.	m.	s.	s.	s.
2	11	15	3	21	20·20	1	10	5·20	1	11	2·87	57·67	+ 0·19
	11	30		21	35·10		10	5·10		11	2·82	57·72	+ 0·24
	11	45		21	50·20		10	5·20		11	2·78	57·58	+ 0·10
	12	15		22	20·10		10	5·10		11	2·70	57·60	+ 0·12
	12	30		22	35·05		10	5·05		11	2·66	57·61	+ 0·13
	12	45		22	50·05		10	5·05		11	2·62	57·57	+ 0·09
	13	15		23	20·00		10	5·00		11	2·54	57·54	+ 0·06
	13	30		23	34·95		10	4·95		11	2·50	57·55	+ 0·07
	13	45		23	50·00		10	5·00		11	2·45	57·45	− 0·03
	14	15		24	19·90		10	4·90		11	2·37	57·47	− 0·01
	14	30		24	34·90		10	4·90		11	2·33	57·43	− 0·05
	14	45		24	49·95		10	4·95		11	2·29	57·34	− 0·14
	15	15		25	19·60		10	4·60		11	2·21	57·61	+ 0·13
	15	30		25	34·55		10	4·55		11	2·17	57·62	+ 0·14
	15	45		25	49·55		10	4·55		11	2·13	57·58	+ 0·10
	16	15		26	19·50		10	4·50		11	2·04	57·54	+ 0·06
	16	30		26	34·50		10	4·50		11	2·00	57·50	+ 0·02
	16	45		26	49·45		10	4·45		11	1·96	57·51	+ 0·03
	17	15		27	19·50		10	4·50		11	1·88	57·38	− 0·10
	17	30		27	34·50		10	4·50		11	1·84	57·34	− 0·14
	17	45		27	49·45		10	4·45		11	1·80	57·35	− 0·13
	18	15		28	19·20		10	4·20		11	1·71	57·51	+ 0·03
	18	30		28	34·40		10	4·40		11	1·67	57·27	− 0·21
	18	45		28	49·20		10	4·20		11	1·63	57·43	− 0·05
2	19	15	3	29	19·10	1	10	4·10	1	11	1·55	57·45	− 0·03

Telegraphic Signals from Madras to Jaffna, 1871, December 15.

Madras Signals.			Jaffna Records.			Difference. Jaff.—Mad.			Relative Correction.			Jaffna West.	Residual Errors.
h.	m.	s.	h.	m.	s.	h.	m.	s.	h.	m.	s.	s.	s.
2	19	30	3	20	34·05	1	10	4·05	1	11	1·51	57·46	− 0·02
	19	45		29	49·05		10	4·05		11	1·47	57·42	− 0·06
	20	15		30	19·00		10	4·00		11	1·38	57·38	− 0·10
	20	30		30	34·00		10	4·00		11	1·34	57·34	− 0·14
2	20	45	3	30	48·95	1	10	3·95	1	11	1·30	57·35	− 0·13
2	16	0·00	3	26	4·60	1	10	4·60	1	11	2·08	57·48	0·95

Telegraphic Signals from Jaffna to Madras, 1871, December 15.

Madras Records.			Jaffna Signals.			Difference. Jaff.—Mad.			Relative Correction.			Jaffna West.	Residual Errors.
h.	m.	s.	h.	m.	s.	h.	m.	s.	h.	m.	s.	s.	s.
2	25	57·3	3	36	0	1	10	2·7	1	11	0·44	57·74	+ 0·01
	26	12·1		36	15		10	2·9		11	0·40	57·50	− 0·23
	26	27·3		36	30		10	2·7		11	0·36	57·66	− 0·07
	26	42·2		36	45		10	2·8		11	0·32	57·52	− 0·21
	27	12·3		37	15		10	2·7		11	0·24	57·54	− 0·19
	27	27·5		37	30		10	2·5		11	0·20	57·70	− 0·03
	27	42·6		37	45		10	2·4		11	0·16	57·76	+ 0·03
	28	12·7		38	15		10	2·3		11	0·08	57·78	+ 0·05
	28	27·7		38	30		10	2·3		11	0·08	57·73	0·00
	28	42·8		38	45		10	2·2		10	59·99	57·79	+ 0·06
	29	13·0		39	15		10	2·0		10	59·91	57·71	− 0·02
	29	28·0		39	30		10	2·0		10	59·87	57·87	+ 0·14
	29	42·8		39	45		10	2·2		10	59·83	57·63	− 0·10
	80	13·0		40	15		10	2·0		10	59·74	57·74	+ 0·01
	30	28·1		40	30		10	1·9		10	59·70	57·80	+ 0·07
	30	43·1		40	45		10	1·9		10	59·66	57·76	+ 0·03
	40	50·9		51	0		10	0·1		10	57·97	57·87	+ 0·14
	41	14·8		51	15		10	0·2		10	57 93	57·73	0·00
	41	29·8		51	30		10	0·2		10	57·89	57·69	− 0·04
	41	45·0	3	51	45	1	10	0·0	1	10	57·84	57·84	+ 0·11

Telegraphic Signals from Jaffna to Madras, 1871, December 15.

Madras Records.			Jaffna Signals.			Difference. Jaff.—Mad.			Relative Correction.			Jaffna West.	Residual Errors.
h.	m.	s.	h.	m.	s.	h.	m.	s.	h.	m.	s.	s.	s.
2	42	15·0	3	52	15	1	10	0·0	1	10	57·76	57·76	+ 0·03
	42	30·0		52	30		10	0·0		10	57·72	57·72	− 0·01
	42	45·1		52	45		9	59·9		10	57·68	57·78	+ 0·05
	43	15·2		53	15		9	59·8		10	57·60	57·80	+ 0·07
	43	30·2		53	30		9	59·8		10	57·56	57·76	+ 0·03
	43	45·3		53	45		9	59·7		10	57·52	57·82	+ 0·09
	44	15·2		54	15		9	59·8		10	57·43	57·63	− 0·10
	44	30·3		54	30		9	59·7		10	57·39	57·69	− 0·04
	44	45·2		54	45		9	59·8		10	57·35	57·55	− 0·18
	45	15·3		55	15		9	59·7		10	57·27	57·57	− 0·16
	45	30·3		55	30		9	59·7		10	57·23	57·53	− 0·20 *.
	45	45·4		55	45		9	59·6		10	57·18	57·58	− 0·15
	46	15·8	•	56	15		9	59·2		10	57·10	57·90	+ 0·17
	46	30·8		56	30		9	59·2		10	57·06	57·36	+ 0·13
	46	45·9		56	45		9	59·1		10	57·02	57·92	+ 0·19
	47	15·9		57	15		9	59·1		10	56·94	57·64	+ 0·11
	47	31·0		57	30		9	59·0		10	56·90	57·90	+ 0·17
	47	46·0		57	45		9	59·0		10	56·86	57·86	+ 0·13
	48	31·0		58	30		9	59·0		10	56·73	57·73	0·00
	48	46·0		58	45		9	59·0		10	56·69	57·69	− 0·04
	49	16·2		59	15		9	58·8		10	56·61	57·81	+ 0·08
	49	31·2		59	30		9	58·8		10	56·57	57·77	+ 0·04
	49	46·2		59	45		9	58·8		10	56·53	57·73	0·00
	50	16·3	4	0	15		9	58·7		10	56·44	57·74	+ 0·01
	50	31·2		0	30		9	58·8		10	56·40	57·60	− 0·13
	50	46·3		0	45		9	58·7		10	56·36	57·66	− 0·07
2	51	1·3	4	1	0	1	9	58·7	1	10	56·32	57·62	− 0·11
2	39	56·08	3	49	56·49	1	10	0·41	1	10	58·14	57·73	0·086

Madras and Jaffna Time Corrections, 1871, *December* 16.

At 1h. 16m. by the Madras Transit Clock, it was 25·32 seconds fast of Sidereal Time, with an adopted daily
rate of 0·92 second gaining.

At 3h. 38m. by Captain Tupman's Chronometer, Muston 610, it was 5h. 13m. 12·69s. slow of Jaffna Mean
Time, with an adopted daily rate of 0·22 second losing.

Hence at 2h. 19m. by the Madras Transit Clock, the relative correction was 1h. 7m. 4·56s. and its
change − 0·16462 second per minute.

Telegraphic Signals from Madras to Jaffna, 1871, *December* 16.

Madras Signals.	Jaffna Records.	Difference. Jaff.—Mad.	Relative Correction.	Jaffna West.	Residual Errors.
h. m. s.	h. m. s.	h. m. s.	h. m. s.	s.	s.
2 15 15	3 21 23·2	1 6 8·2	1 7 5·18	56·98	− 0·14
15 30	21 38·2	6 8·2	7 5·14	56·94	− 0·18
15 45	21 53·0	6 8·0	7 5·10	57·10	− 0·02
16 15	22 23·2	6 8·2	7 5·01	56·81	− 0·31
16 45	22 52·9	6 7·9	7 4·93	57·03	− 0·09
17 15	23 22·7	6 7·7	7 4·85	57·15	+ 0·03
17 30	23 37·7	6 7·7	7 4·81	57·11	− 0·01
17 45	23 52·7	6 7·7	7 4·77	57·07	− 0·05
18 15	24 22·5	6 7·5	7 4·68	57·18	+ 0·16
18 30	24 37·5	6 7·5	7 4·64	57·14	+ 0·02
18 45	24 52·5	6 7·5	7 4·60	57·10	− 0·12
19 15	25 22·3	6 7·3	7 4·52	57·22	+ 0·10
19 30	25 37·3	6 7·3	7 4·48	57·18	+ 0·06
19 45	25 52·2	6 7·2	7 4·44	57·24	+ 0·12
20 15	26 22·2	6 7·2	7 4·35	57·15	+ 0·03
20 30	26 37·1	6 7·1	7 4·31	57·21	+ 0·19
20 45	26 52·1	6 7·1	7 4·27	57·17	+ 0·05
21 15	27 22·0	6 7·0	7 4·19	57·19	+ 0·07
21 30	27 37·0	6 7·0	7 4·15	57·15	+ 0·13
21 45	27 52·0	6 7·0	7 4·11	57·11	− 0·01
22 15	28 22·0	6 7·0	7 4·03	27·03	− 0·09
22 30	28 36·9	6 6·9	7 3·98	57·08	− 0·04
22 45	28 51·8	6 6·8	7 3·94	57·14	+ 0·02
23 15	29 21·7	6 6·7	7 3·86	57·16	+ 0·04
23 45	29 51·6	6 6·6	7 3·78	57·18	+ 0·06
24 15	30 21·5	6 6·5	7 3·70	57·20	+ 0·08
24 30	30 36·5	6 6·5	7 3·66	57·16	+ 0·04
2 24 45	3 30 51·5	1 6 6·5	1 7 3·61	57·11	− 0·11

Means of Signals from Madras to Jaffna, 1871, Dec. 16.

Madras Signals.	Jaffna Records.	Difference. Jaff.—Mad.	Relative Correction.	Jaffna West.	Residual Errors.
h. m. s.	h. m. s.	h. m. s.	h. m. s.	s.	s.
2 20 0·00	3 26 7·28	1 6 7·28	1 7 4·40	57·12	0·065

Telegraphic Signals from Jaffna to Madras, 1871, December 16.

Madras Records.	Jaffna Signals.	Difference. Jaff.—Mad.	Relative Correction.	Jaffna West.	Residual Errors.
h. m. s.	h. m. s.	h. m. s.	h. m. s.	s.	s.
2 27 9·1	3 33 15	1 6 5·9	1 7 3·23	57·33	+ 0·05
27 24·2	33 30	6 5·8	7 3·18	57·38	+ 0·10
27 30·1	33 45	6 5·9	7 3·14	57·24	− 0·04
28 9·2	34 15	6 5·8	7 3·05	57·25	− 0·03
28 24·3	34 30	6 5·7	7 3·01	57·31	+ 0·03
38 39·2	34 45	6 5·8	7 2·97	57·17	− 0·11
29 9·4	35 15	6 5·6	7 2·89	57·29	+ 0·01
29 24·5	35 30	6 5·5	7 2·85	57·35	+ 0·07
29 39·5	35 45	6 5·5	7 2·81	57·31	+ 0·03
30 9·6	36 15	6 5·4	7 2·72	57·32	+ 0·04
30 24·5	36 30	6 5·5	7 2·68	57·18	− 0·10
30 39·6	36 45	6 5·4	7 2·64	57·24	− 0·04
31 9·7	37 15	6 5·3	7 2·56	57·26	− 0·02
31 24·8	37 30	6 5·2	7 2·52	57·32	+ 0·04
31 40·0	37 45	6 5·0	7 2·48	57·48	+ 0·20
32 10·0	38 15	6 5·0	7 2·39	57·39	+ 0·11
32 25·0	38 30	6 5·0	7 2·35	57·35	+ 0·07
32 40·0	38 45	6 5·0	7 2·31	57·31	+ 0·03
33 10·1	39 15	6 4·9	7 2·23	57·33	+ 0·05
33 25·0	39 30	6 5·0	7 2·19	57·19	− 0·09
33 40·2	39 45	6 4·8	7 2·14	·57·34	+ 0·06
34 10·1	40 15	6 4·9	7 2·06	57·10	− 0·12
34 25·2	40 30	6 4·8	7 2·02	57·22	− 0·06
34 40·3	40 45	6 4·7	7 1·98	57·28	0·00
35 10·4	41 15	6 4·6	7 1·90	57·30	+ 0·02
35 25·4	41 30	6 4·6	7 1·86	57·26	− 0·02
35 40·4	41 45	6 4·6	7 1·81	57·21	− 0·07
36 10·6	42 15	6 4·4	7 1·73	57·33	+ 0·05
36 25·5	42 30	6 4·5	7 1·69	57·19	− 0·09
2 36 40·5	3 42 45	1 6 4·5	1 7 1·65	57·15	− 0·13

Means of Signals from Jaffna to Madras, 1871, December 16.

Madras Records.	Jaffna Signals.	Difference. Jaff.—Mad.	Relative Correction.	Jaffna West.	Residual Errors.
h. m. s.	h. m. s.	h. m. s.	h. m. s.	s.	s.
2 . 31 54·85	3 38 0·00	1 6 5·15	1 7 2·43	57·28	0·063

Summary of Telegraphic Results.

1871.	Number of Signals.	Jaffna West.	Probable Errors.	Compound Retardation.
		s.	s.	s.
December 15 ...	By 30 from Madras ...	57·48	± 0·015	0·125
„ „ ...	By 47 from Jaffna ...	57·73	± 0·011	
„ 16 ...	By 28 from Madras ...	57·12	± 0·014	0·070
„ „ ..	By 30 from Jaffna	57·28	± 0·010	

Final Results.

	h.	m.	s.
Madras Observatory East of Greenwich. ...	5	20	59·40
Jaffna Fort West of Madras.			57·40
Jaffna Fort East of Greenwich.	5	20	2·00
Probable Error of Signals and Madras Transits..		±	0·034
Retardation. (Current and Instruments.) ...			0·097

COLOMBO.

The longitude of Colombo, like that of Jaffna, was determined by desire of Captain J. L. Tupman, R. M. A., in connection with the total eclipse of the Sun on 1871, December 11th, the arrangements being much the same on both occasions. Signals were exchanged on three nights between Madras and Colombo by Captain Tupman and myself and I believe with results to our mutual satisfaction. The geographical point of reference at Colombo was the Flagstaff, behind the Governor's Residence. At both Jaffna and Colombo Captain Tupman expressed his great obligation for the willing aid rendered him by G. Moberly, Esq., the Government Telegraph official who had to assist him in all necessary electrical requirements, and I have always had a similar acknowledgment to make from my own experience in all cases in which the help of the Telegraph Department was needed.

Local Sidereal and Mean Time Determinations.

MADRAS.				COLOMBO.
Star.	Transit Clock.	Sidereal Correction.	Residual Errors.	Mean Time Chronometer, Muston 610.
1871, December 31.				1871, December 30.
	h. m.	s.	s.	
67 Ceti	2 10	− 39·47	− 0·02	By five double altitudes of the Sun's upper limb, and five more of the lower limb, taken with the same instruments and precautions used at Jaffna, the Chronometer was 5h. 12m. 37·33s. slow when it shewed 15h. 15m., corresponding to 20h. 27m. of Colombo Mean Time.
ξ² Ceti	2 22	− 39·53	− 0·07	
γ Ceti	2 37	− 39·44	+ 0·03	
a Ceti	2 56	− 39·58	− 0·10	
ν Orionis......	6 1	− 39·58	+ 0·02	
μ Geminorum	6 16	− 39·31	+ 0·30	1872, January 2.
γ Geminorum.	6 31	− 39·78	− 0·16	By six double altitudes of the Sun's lower limb and six more of the upper limb, taken as before, the Chronometer was 5h. 12m, 38·46s. slow when it shewed 22h. 56m., corresponding to 4h. 8m. of Colombo Mean Time.
Means	4 8	− 39·53	0·100	

Probable error of mean correction ...... ± 0·024

Adopted daily change.............................. − 0·93

Local Sidereal and Mean Time Determinations.

MADRAS.				COLOMBO.
Star.	Transit Clock.	Sidereal Correction.	Residual Errors.	Mean Time Chronometer Muston 610.
	1872, January 4.			1872, January 3, 4.
	h. m.	s.	s.	
ν Piscium ...	1 35	− 43·36	+ 0·06	
β Arietis......	1 48	− 43·30	− 0·07	By six double altitudes of the Sun's lower limb, and six more of the upper limb, taken as before, the Chronometer shewing 15h. 13m., corresponding to December 3rd 20h. 26m., and two similar afternoon sets, at Chronometer time 22h. 24m., corresponding to December 4th 3h. 36m.; the combined results gave the Chronometer 5h. 12m. 40s. slow, when it shewed 18h. 48m., corresponding to December 4th 1h. 7m. of Colombo Mean Time.
67 Ceti	2 11	− 43·27	− 0·02	
ξ² Ceti..........	2 22	− 43·23	+ 0·02	
γ Ceti..........	2 37	− 43·26	0·00	
δ Arietis	3 5	− 43·18	+ 0·10	
ι Aurigæ......	4 49	− 43·42	− 0·07	
δ Orionis......	5 26	− 43·29	+ 0·08	
Betelgeux.....	5 49	− 43·30	+ 0·09	
Means..........	3 18	− 43·29	0·055	

Probable error of mean correction.......... ± 0·016

Adopted daily change........................... − 0·91

	1872, January 5.			1872, January 4, 5.
Aldebaran....	4 29	− 44·37	− 0·05	By twenty-four double altitudes of the Sun, taken about the same times before and after noon as yesterday, the Chronometer was 5h. 12m. 41·10s. slow, when it shewed 18h. 48m., corresponding to December 5th 0h. 1m. of Colombo Mean Time.
ι Aurigæ.......	4 49	− 44·29	+ 0·04	
ε Leporis......	5 1	− 44·35	− 0·01	
β Tauri........	5 19	− 44·32	+ 0·03	
δ Orionis......	5 26	− 44·34	+ 0·02	
ε Orionis......	5 30	− 44·35	+ 0·01	
α Columbæ...	5 36	− 44·36	0·00	1872, January 5, 6.
Betelgeux.....	5 49	− 44·42	− 0·05	By twenty-four double altitudes of the Sun, taken before and after noon as on the two previous days, the Chronometer was 5h. 12m. 41·94s. slow, when it shewed 18h. 48m., corresponding to December 6th 0h. 1m. of Colombo Mean Time.
Mean..........	5 15	− 44·35	0·026	

Probable error of mean correction...... ± 0·008

Adopted daily change.......................... − 0·95

Madras and Colombo Time Corrections, 1871, December 31.

At 4h. 8m. by the Madras Transit Clock, it was 39·53 seconds fast of Sidereal Time, with an adopted daily rate of 0·03 second gaining.

At 3h. 59m. by Captain Tupman's Chronometer, Muston 610, it was 5h. 12m. 37·59s. slow of Colombo Mean Time, with an adopted daily rate of 0·49 second losing.

Hence at 4h. 39m. by the Madras Transit Clock, the relative correction was 8m. 3·87s. and its change − 0·16481 second per minute.

Telegraphic Signals from Colombo to Madras, 1871, December 31.

Madras Records.			Colombo Signals.			Difference. Col.—Mad.		Relative Correction.		Colombo West.		Residual Errors.
h.	m.	s.	h.	m.	s.	m.	s.	m.	s.	m.	s.	s.
3	51	40·7	3	58	15	6	34·3	8	11·67	1	37·37	+ 0·10
	51	55·5		58	30	6	34·5	8	11·63	1	37·13	− 0·14
	52	10·7		58	45	6	34·3	8	11·59	1	37·29	+ 0·02
	52	41·0		59	15	6	34·0	8	11·50	1	37·50	+ 0·23
	53	11·0		59	45	6	34·0	8	11·42	1	37·42	+ 0·15
	53	41·0	4	0	15	6	34·0	8	11·34	1	37·34	+ 0·07
	53	56·0		0	30	6	34·0	8	11·30	1	37·30	+ 0·03
	54	11·1		0	45	6	33·9	8	11·25	1	37·35	+ 0·08
	54	41·0		1	15	6	34·0	8	11·17	1	37·17	− 0·10
	54	56·1		1	30	6	33·9	8	11·13	1	37·23	− 0·04
	55	11·1		1	45	6	33·9	8	11·09	1	37·19	− 0·08
	55	41·2		2	15	6	33·8	8	11·01	1	37·21	− 0·06
	55	56·2		2	30	6	33·8	8	10·97	1	37·17	− 0·10
	56	11·3		2	45	6	33·7	8	10·93	1	37·23	− 0·04
	56	41·4		3	15	6	33·6	8	10·84	1	37·24	− 0·03
	57	11·5		3	45	6	33·5	8	10·76	1	37·26	− 0·01
	57	41·5		4	15	6	33·5	8	10·68	1	37·18	− 0·09
	58	41·7		5	15	6	33·3	8	10·51	1	37·21	− 0·06
	58	57·0		5	30	6	33·0	8	10·47	1	37·47	+ 0·20
	59	12·0		5	45	6	33·0	8	10·43	1	37·43	+ 0·16
	59	42·0		6	15	6	33·0	8	10·35	1	37·35	+ 0·08
4	0	12·0		6	45	6	33·0	8	10·26	1	37·26	− 0·01
	0	42·0		7	15	6	33·0	8	10·18	1	37·18	− 0·09
	0	57·2		7	30	6	32·8	8	10·14	1	37·34	+ 0·07
	1	12·1		7	45	6	32·9	8	10·10	1	37·20	− 0·07
4	1	27·0	4	8	0	6	33·0	8	10·06	1	37·06	− 0·21
3	56	29·28	4	3	2·88	6	33·60	8	10·87	1	37·27	0·089

Telegraphic Signals from Madras to Colombo, 1871, December 31.

Madras Signals.			Colombo Records.			Difference. Col.—Mad.		Relative Correction.		Colombo West.		Residual Errors.
h.	m.	s.	h.	m.	s.	m.	s.	m.	s.	m.	s.	s.
4	30	0	4	36	28·0	6	28·0	8	5·35	1	37·35	+ 0·31
	30	15		36	43·5	6	28·5	8	5·31	1	36·81	− 0·23
	30	30		36	58·2	6	28·2	8	5·27	1	37·07	+ 0·03
	30	45		37	13·2	6	.28·2	8	5·23	1	37·03	− 0·01
	31	15		37	43·1	6	28·1	8	5·15	1	37·05	+ 0·01
	31	30		37	58·1	6	28·1	8	5·11	1	37·01	− 0·03
	31	45		38	13·1	6	28·1	8	5·07	1	36·97	− 0·07
	36	15		42	42·2	6	27·2	8	4·32	1	37·12	+ 0·08
	36	30		42	57·4	6·	27·4	8	4·28	1	36·88	− 0·16
	36	45		43	12·3	6	27·3	8	4·24	1	36·94	− 0·10
	37	15		43	42·1	6	27·1	8	4·16	1	37·06	+ 0·02
	37	30		43	57·1	6	27·1	8	4·12	1	37·02	− 0·02
	37	45		44	12·1	6	27·1	8	4·08	1	36·98	− 0·06
	38	15		44	42·1	6	27·1	8	3·99	1	36·89	− 0·15
	38	30		44	57·0	6	27·0	8	3·95	1	36·95	− 0·09
	38	45		45	12·0	6	27·0	8	3·91	1	36·91	− 0·13
	39	15		45	41·8	6	26·8	8	3·83	1	37·03	− 0·01
	39	30		45	56·7	6	26·7	8	3·79	1	37·09	+ 0·05
5	6	0	5	12	22·5	6	22·5	7	59·42	1	36·92	− 0·12
	6	15		12	37·2	6	22·2	7	59·38	1	37·18	+ 0·14
	6	30		12	52·3	6	22·3	7	59·34	1	37·04	0·00
	6	45		13	7·1	6	22·1	7	59·30	1	37·20	+ 0·16
	7	15		13	37·1	6	22·1	7	59·21	1	37·11	+ 0·07
	7	30		13	52·1	6	22·1	7	59·17	1	37·07	+ 0·03
	8	15		14	37·0	6	22·0	7	59·05	1	37·05	+ 0·01
	8	30		14	52·0	6	22·0	7	59·01	1	37·01	− 0·03
	8	45		15	7·0	6	22·0	7	58·97	1	36·97	− 0·07
	9	15		15	36·6	6	21·6	7	58·88	1	37·28	+ 0·24
	9	30		15	51·7	6	21·7	7	58·84	1	37·14	+ 0·10
5	9	45	5	16	6·7	6	21·7	7	58·80	1	37·10	+ 0·06
4	48	13·00	4	54	38·31	6	25·31	8	2·35	1	37·04	0·079

Madras and Colombo Time Corrections, 1872, January 4.

At 3h. 18m. by the Madras Transit Clock, it was 43·20 seconds fast of Sidereal Time, with an adopted daily rate of 0·91 second gaining.

At 3h. 54m. by Captain Tupman's Chronometer, Muston 610, it was 5h. 12m. 40·57s. slow of Colombo Mean Time, with an adopted daily rate of 0·85 second losing.

Hence at 4h. 1m. by the Madras Transit Clock, the relative correction was 7m. 40· 7s. and its change + 0·16505 second per minute.

Telegraphic Signals from Colombo to Madras, 1872, January 4.

Madras Records.			Colombo Signals.			Difference. Col.—Mad.		Relative Correction.		Colombo West.		Residual Errors.
h.	m.	s.	h.	m.	s.	m.	s.	m.	s.	m.	s.	s.
3	51	31·3	3	42	15	9	16·3	7	38·71	1	37·59	− 0·16
	51	46·2		42	30	9	16·2	7	38·75	1	37·45	− 0·30
	52	1·2		42	45	9	16·2	7	38·79	1	37·41	− 0·34
	52	31·6		43	15	9	16·6	7	38·87	1	37·73	− 0·02
	52	46·6		43	30	9	16·6	7	38·91	1	37·69	− 0·06
	53	1·9		43	45	9	16·9	7	38·95	1	37·95	+ 0·20
	53	32·0		44	15	9	17·0	7	39·04	1	37·96	+ 0·21
	53	47·0		44	30	9	17·0	7	39·08	1	37·92	+ 0·17
	54	2·0		44	45	9	17·0	7	39·12	1	37·88	+ 0·13
	54	32·0		45	15	9	17·0	7	39·20	1	37·80	+ 0·05
	54	47·1		45	30	9	17·1	7	39·24	1	37·86	+ 0·11
	55	2·0		45	45	9	17·0	7	39·28	1	37·72	− 0·03
	55	32·1		46	15	9	17·1	7	39·37	1	37·73	− 0·02
	55	47·2		46	30	9	17·2	7	39·41	1	37·79	+ 0·04
	56	2·1		46	45	9	17·1	7	39·45	1	37·65	− 0·10
	56	32·3		47	15	9	17·3	7	39·53	1	37·77	+ 0·02
	56	47·2		47	30	9	17·2	7	39·57	1	37·63	− 0·12
	57	2·4		47	45	9	17·4	7	39·62	1	37·78	+ 0·03
	57	32·4		48	15	9	17·4	7	39·70	1	37·70	− 0·05
	57	47·4		48	30	9	17·4	7	39·74	1	37·66	− 0·09
	58	2·5		48	45	9	17·5	7	39·78	1	37·72	− 0·03
	58	32·6		49	15	9	17·6	7	39·86	1	37·74	− 0·01
	58	47·7		49	30	9	17·7	7	39·91	1	37·79	+ 0·04
	59	2·5		49	45	9	17·5	7	39·95	1	37·55	− 0·20
	59	33·0		50	15	9	18·0	7	40·03	1	37·97	+ 0·22
	59	47·9		50	30	9	17·9	7	40·07	1	37·83	+ 0·08
4	0	3·0		50	45	9	18·0	7	40·11	1	37·89	+ 0·14
	0	33·0		51	15	9	18·0	7	40·20	1	37·80	+ 0·05
	0	48·0		51	30	9	18·0	7	40·24	1	37·76	+ 0·01
4	1	3·1	3	51	45	9	18·1	7	40·28	1	37·82	+ 0·07
3	56	17·24	3	47	0·00	9	17·24	7	39·49	1	37·75	0·103

Telegraphic Signals from Madras to Colombo, 1872, January 4.

Madras Signals.			Colombo Records.			Difference. Col.—Mad.		Relative Correction.		Colombo West.		Residual Errors.
h.	m.	s.	h.	m.	s.	m.	s.	m.	s.	m.	s.	s.
4	4	0	3	54	41·8	9	18·2	7	40·77	1	37·43	− 0·09
	4	15		54	56·7	9	18·3	7	40·81	1	37·49	− 0·03
	4	30		55	11·7	9	18·3	7	40·85	1	37·45	− 0·07
	4	45		55	26·6	9	18·4	7	40·89	1	37·51	− 0·01
	5	15		55	50·6·	9	18·4	7	40·97	1	37·43	− 0·09
	5	30		56	11·5	9	18·5	7	41·01	1	37·49	− 0·03
	5	45		56	26·5	9	18·5	7	41·05	1	37·45	− 0·07
	6	15		56	56·4	9	18·6	7	41·14	1	37·46	− 0·06
	6	30		57	11·2	9	18·8	7	41·18	1	37·62	+ 0·10
	6	45		57	26·2	9	18·8	7	41·22	1	37·58	+ 0·06
	7	15		57	56·1	9	18·9	7	41·30	1	37·60	+ 0·08
	7	30		58	11·1	9	18·9	7	41·34	1	37·56	+ 0·04
	7	45		58	26·0	9	19·0	7	41·38	1	37·62	+ 0·10
	8	15		58	56·0	9	19·0	7	41·47	1	37·53	+ 0·01
	8	30		59	11·0	9	19·0	7	41·51	1	37·49	− 0·03
	8	45		59	26·0	9	19·0	7	41·55	1	37·45	− 0·07
	9	15		59	55·9	9	19·1	7	41·63	1	37·47	− 0·05
	9	30	4	0	10·8	9	19·2	7	41·67	1	37·53	+ 0·01
	9	45		0	25·7	9	19·3	7	41·71	1	37·59	+ 0·07
	10	15		0	55·6	9	19·4	7	41·80	1	37·60	+ 0·08
	10	30		1	10·6	9	19·4	7	41·84	1	37·56	+ 0·04
	10	45		1	25·6	9	19·4	7	41·88	1	37·52	0·00
	11	15		1	55·5	9	19·5	7	41·96	1	37·54	+ 0·02
	11	30		2	10·5	9	19·5	7	42·00	1	37·50	− 0·02
	11	45		2	25·5	9	19·5	7	42·04·	1	37·46	− 0·06
	12	15		2	55·4	9	19·6	7	42·13	1	37·47	− 0·05
	12	30		3	10·4	9	19·6	7	42·17	1	37·43	− 0·09
	12	45		3	25·2	9	19·8	7	42·21	1	37·59	+ 0·07
	13	15		3	55·1	9	19·9	7	42·29	1	37·61	+ 0·09
	13	30		4	10·1	9	19·9	7	42·33	1	37·57	+ 0·05
4	13	45	4	4	25·1	9	19·9	7	42·37	1	37·53	+ 0·01
4	8	50·32	3	59	31·24	9	19·08	7	41·56	1	37·52	0·053

Madras and Colombo Time. Corrections, 1872, January 5.

At 5h. 15m. by the Madras Transit Clock, it was 44·35 seconds fast of Sidereal Time, with an adopted daily rate of 0·95 seconds gaining.

At 4h. 14m. by Captain Tupman's Chronometer, Muston 610, it was 5h. 12m. 41·43s. slow of Colombo. Mean Time, with an adopted daily rate of 0·84 second losing.

Hence at 4h. 45m. by the Madras Transit Clock, the relative correction was 11m. 45·27s. and its change + 0·16507 second per minute.

Telegraphic Signals from Colombo to Madras, 1872, Jan. 5.

Madras Records.			Colombo Signals.			Difference. Col.—Mad.		Relative Correction.		Colombo West.		Residual Errors.
h.	m.	s.	h.	m.	s.	m.	s.	m.	s.	m.	s.	s.
3	50	14·0	3	37	0	13	14·0	11	36·23	1	37·77	+ 0·05
	50	29·0		37	15	13	14·0	11	36·27	1	37·73	+ 0·01
	50	44·0		37	30	13	14·0	11	36·31	1	37·09	− 0·03*,
	50	59·1		37	45	13	14·1	11	36·35	1	37·75	+ 0·03
	51	29·2		38	15	13	14·2	11	36·44	1	37·76	+ 0·04
	51	44·1		38	30	13	14·1	11	36·48	1	37·02	− 0·10
	51	59·3		38	45	13	14·3	11	36·52	1	37·78	+ 0·06
	52	29·4		39	15	13	14·4	11	36·60	1	37·80	+ 0·08
	52	44·6		39	30	13	14·0	11	36·65	1	37·95	+ 0·23
	52	59·4		39	45	13	14·4	11	36·69	1	37·71	− 0·01
	53	29·5		40	15	13	14·5	11	36·77	1	37·73	+ 0·01
	53	44·5		40	30	13	14·5	11	36·81	1	37·69	− 0·03
	53	59·6		40	45	13	14·6	11	36·85	1	37·75	+ 0·03
	54	44·5		41	30	13	14·5	11	36·97	1	37·53	− 0·19
	54	59·5		41	45	13	14·5	11	37·02	1	37·48	− 0·24
	55	30·0		42	15	13	15·0	11	37·10	1	37·90	+ 0·18
	55	44·9		42	30	13	14·9	11	37·14	1	37·76	+ 0·04
	56	0·0		42	45	13	15·0	11	37·18	1	37·82	+ 0·10
	56	30·0		43	15	13	15·0	11	37·26	1	37·74	+ 0·02
	56	45·0		43	30	13	15·0	11	37·30	1	37·70	− 0·02
	57	0·0		43	45	13	15·0	11	37·35	1	37·65	− 0·07
	57	30·2		44	15	13	15·2	11	37·43	1	37·77	+ 0·05
	57	45·1		44	30	13	15·1	11	37·47	1	37·63	− 0·09
	58	0·2		44	45	13	15·2	11	37·51	1	37·69	− 0·03
	58	30·4		45	15	13	15·4	11	37·59	1	37·81	+ 0·09
	58	45·3		45	30	13	15·3	11	37·64	1	37·66	− 0·06
	59	0·3		45	45	13	15·3·	11	37·68	1	37·62	− 0·10
	59	30·5		46	15	13	15·5	11	37·76	1	37·74	+ 0·02
	59	45·5		46	30	13	15·5	11	37·80	1	37·70	− 0·02
4	0	0·5	3	46	45	13	15·5	11	37·84	1	37·66	− 0·06
3	55	6·25	3	41	51·50	13	14·75	11	37·03	1	37·72	0·070

Telegraphic Signals from Madras to Colombo, 1872, January 5.

Madras Signals.			Colombo Records.			Difference. Col.—Mad.		Relative Correction.		Colombo West.		Residual Errors.
h.	m.	s.	h.	m.	s.	m.	s.	m.	s.	m.	s.	s.
4	2	0	3	48	44·5	13	15·5	11	38·17	1	37·33	− 0·01
	2	15		48	59·5	13	15·5	11	38·21	1	37·29	− 0·05
	2	30		49	14·5	13	15·5	11	38·26	1	37·24	− 0·10
	2	45		49	29·4	13	15·6	11	38·30	1	37·30	− 0·04
	3	15		49	59·2	13	15·8	11	38·38	1	37·42	+ 0·08
	3	30		50	14·1	13	15·9	11	38·42	1	37·48	+ 0·14
	3	45		50	29·1	13	15·9	11	38·46	1	37·44	+ 0·10
	4	15		50	59·1	13	15·9	11	38·54	1	37·36	+ 0·02
	4	30		51	14·1	13	15·9	11	38·58	1	37·32	− 0·02
	4	45		51	29·0	13	16·0	11	38·63	1	37·37	+ 0·03
	5	15		51	59·0	13	16·0	11	38·71	1	37·29	− 0·05
	5	30		52	14·0	13	16·0	11	38·75	1	37·25	− 0·09
	5	45		52	28·9	13	16·1	11	38·79	1	37·31	− 0·03
	6	15		52	58·8	13	16·2	11	38·87	1	37·33	− 0·01
	6	30		53	13·7	13	16·3	11	38·91	1	37·39	+ 0·05
	6	45		53	28·6	13	16·4	11	38·96	1	37·44	+ 0·10
	7	15		53	58·6	13	16·4	11	39·04	1	37·36	+ 0·02
	7	45		54	28·5	13	16·5	11	39·12	1	37·38	+ 0·04
	8	15		54	58·5	13	16·5	11	39·20	1	37·30	− 0·04
	8	30		55	13·5	13	16·5	11	39·24	1	37·26	− 0·08
	8	45		55	28·4	13	16·6	11	39·29	1	37·31	− 0·03
	9	15		55	58·3	13	16·7	11	39·37	1	37·33	− 0·01
	9	30		56	13·2	13	16·8	11	39·41	1	37·39	+ 0·05
	9	45		56	28·2	13	16·8	11	39·45	1	37·35	+ 0·01
	10	15		56	58·1	13	16·9	11	39·53	1	37·37	+ 0·03
	10	30		57	13·1	13	16·9	11	39·57	1	37·33	− 0·01
	10	45		57	28·0	13	17·0	11	39·62	1	37·38	+ 0·04
	11	15		57	58·0	13	17·0	11	39·70	1	37·30	− 0·04
	11	30		58	13·0	13	17·0	11	39·74	1	37·26	− 0·08
	11	45		58	27·9	13	17·1	11	39·78	1	37·32	− 0·02
4	12	0	3	58	42·8	13	17·2	11	39·82	1	37·38	+ 0·04
4	6	59·08	3	53	42·70	13	16·33	11	38·99	1	37·34	0·047

Summary of Telegraphic Results.

1871-72.	Number of Signals.	Colombo West.	Probable Errors.	Compound Retardation.
		m. *s.*	*s.*	*s.*
December 31 ...	By 26 from Colombo	1 37·27	± 0·015	
				0·115
,, ,, ...	By 30 from Madras ...	1 37·04	± 0·012	
January 4 ...	By 30 from Colombo	1 37·75	± 0·016	
				0·115
,, ,, ...	By 31 from Madras ...	1 37·52	± 0·008	
,, 5 ..	By 30 from Colombo	1 37·72	± 0·011	
				0·190
,, ,, ...	By 31 from Madras ...	1 37·34	± 0·007	

Final Results.

	h.	m.	s.
Madras Observatory East of Greenwich	5	20	59·40
Colombo Flagstaff West of Madras.		1	37·44
Colombo Flagstaff East of Greenwich.	5	19	21·96
Probable Error of Signals and Madras Transits...			± 0·020
Retardation. (Current and Instruments.) ...			0·140

KARACHI.

The telegraphic determination of the difference of longitude between Madras Observatory and Karachi was of two-fold importance and interest, from its being one of the Indian stations at which observations of the Transit of Venus, on 1874 December 8th, were arranged to be made; and still more as a means of comparison between Madras and Greenwich, in conjunction with the similar operations by Drs. Becker and Fritsch, members of the German Transit of Venus Expedition to Ispahan. A severe test of the accuracy of both determinations is furnished by the consideration, that the resulting longitude of Madras, as found, viâ Karachi, Ispahan and Berlin, is only one-tenth of a second less than that now adopted from the far more elaborate processes employed by Lieut.-Col. Campbell and Major Heaviside, R. E., Officers of the Great Trigonometrical Survey of India, between Madras, Bombay, Aden and Suez, in 1877; combined with those between Suez, Mokattam and Greenwich, by Lord Lindsay's "Transit of Venus" party in 1874.

The observer and operator at Karachi was General T. Addison, c.b., then in command of the Poona Division. His observatory was connected by triangulation with that of the Great Trigonometrical Survey, on Bath Island, and the latter was found to be 0·60 second further West of Madras. Not being aware whether any permanent mark of the site of General Addison's temporary station was made, I have thought it better to refer the final result to the G. T. S. Observatory; the locality of which is necessarily a definite geographical position in the Survey.

Telegraphic exchanges, of one hundred signals each way, were made on December 15th, without a single mistake throughout on either side. Both star transits and telegraphic signals were recorded on the chronograph at Karachi, and the tape fillets, as well as their tabulated records, were all in my possession before the end of the month; mine to General Addison following early in January. Prompt completion of such works greatly adds to the interest felt in them by the operators, but is rarely possible in India. It is surprising, that with only three clock stars at Karachi such accuracy should have been attained; but limited time and unfavorable weather prevented General Addison from getting more. As usual, the most willing aid was rendered at each end by the officers of the Government Telegraph Department; Mr. W. Williams at Karachi, and Mr. W. F. Melhuish at Madras.

Local Sidereal Time Determinations, 1874, December 13.

MADRAS.				KARACHI.
Star.	Transit Clock.	Sidereal Correction.	Residual Errors.	
	h. m.	s.	s.	
θ Ceti.........	1 18	− 10·07	− 0·06	Sidereal Time determined by three stars only, *viz.*, α Andromedæ, μ Geminorum and δ Leonis; using a portable Transit Instrument, an electrical clock, and a tape recording chronograph. No details were furnished except the interpolated corrections to clock times of signals, the first and last being :
η Piscium	1 25	− 9·99	+ 0·02	
ν Piscium	1 35	− 10·24	− 0·22	
β Arietis......	1 48	− 10·07	− 0·05	
α Arietis	2 0	− 9·91	+ 0·12	h. m. s. s.
67 Ceti.........	2 11	− 9·94	+ 0·10	At 4 30 59.........Correction......... + 9·500
γ² Ceti.........	2 37	− 10·07	− 0·02	'At 5 19 50.........Correction......... + 9·584 *.*
α Ceti	2 56	− 10·13	− 0·07	
α Persei........	3 16	− 10·08	− 0·01	
γ¹ Eridani....	3 52	− 9·90	+ 0·10	
Means.........	2 18	− 10·04	0·086	

Probable error of mean correction   ...   ± 0·024

Adopted daily change   ...   .   − 0·83

Comparisons of Madras Clocks and Chronometer.

Transit Clock.	Sidereal Correction.	Chronometer Dent 1068.	Mean Time Correction.	Shepherd's Electrical Clock.	Mean Time Correction.
h. m. s.	s.	1874. h. m. s.	m. s.	h. m. s.	s.
0 49 16	− 9·99	Dec. 13... 7 22 29·5	− 1 43·60	......	......
......	......	„ „ ... 11 24 43·0	− 1 43·88	11 23 0	− 0·88
8 59 17	− 10·27	„ „ ... 15 31 10·5	− 1 44·16	......	......
......	......	„ „ ... 22 40 43·5	− 1 44·66	22 30 0	− 1·16

Madras and Karachi Time Corrections, 1874, December 13.

At 11h. 25m. by Shepherd's Electrical Clock, it was 0·88 second fast of Madras Mean Time, with an adopted daily rate of 0·60 second gaining.

At 4h. 31m. by General Addison's Transit Clock, it was 9·50 seconds slow of Karachi Sidereal Time with an adopted daily rate of 2·47 seconds losing.

Hence at 12h. 13m. by Shepherd's Electrical Clock, the relative correction was 6h. 31m. 2·31s. and its change — 0·16215 second per minute.

Telegraphic Signals from Madras to Karachi, 1874, December 13.

Madras Signals.			Karachi Records.			Difference. Kar.—Mad.			Relative Correction.			Karachi West.		Residual Errors.
h.	m.	s.	h.	m.	s.	h.	m.	s.	h.	m.	s.	m.	s.	s.
11	55	10	4	30	59·04	7	24	10·96	6	31	5·20	53	5·76	+ 0·02
	55	20		31	9·08		24	10·92		31	5·17	53	5·75	+ 0·01
	55	30		31	19·19		24	10·81		31	5·15	53	5·66	− 0·08
	55	40		31	29·19		24	10·81		31	5·12	53	5·69	− 0·05
	55	50		31	39·30		24	10·70		31	5·09	53	5·01	− 0·13
	56	10		31	59·18		24	10·82		31	5·04	53	5·78	+ 0·04
	56	20		32	9·33		24	10·67		31	5·01	53	5·66	− 0·08
	56	30		32	19·31		24	10·69		31	4·98	53	5·71	− 0·03
	56	40		32	29·34		24	10·66		31	4·96	53	5·70	− 0·04
	56	50		32	39·38		24	10·62		31	4·93	53	5·69	− 0·05
	57	10		32	59·44		24	10·56		31	4·88	53	5·68	− 0·06
	57	20		33	9·48		24	10·52		31	4·85	53	5·07	− 0·07
	57	30		33	19·48		24	10·52		31	4·82	53	5·70	− 0·04
	57	40		33	29·45		24	10·55		31	4·79	53	5·76	+ 0·02
	57	50		33	39·40		24	10·60		31	4·77	53	5·83	+ 0·09
	58	10		33	59·51		24	10·49		31	4·71	53	5·78	+ 0·04
	58	20		34	9·51		24	10·49		31	4·69	53	5·80	+ 0·06
	58	30		34	19·58		24	10·42		31	4·66	53	5·76	+ 0·02
	58	40		34	29·61		24	10·39		31	4·63	53	5·76	+ 0·02
	58	50		34	39·07		24	10·33		31	4·61	53	5·72	− 0·02
	59	10		34	59·71		24	10·29		31	4·55	53	5·74	0·00
	59	20		35	9·76		24	10·24		31	4·52	53	5·72	− 0·02
	59	30		35	19·71		24	10·29		31	4·50	53	5·79	+ 0·05
	59	40		35	29·76		24	10·24		31	4·47	53	5·77	+ 0·03
	59	50		35	39·78		24	10·22		31	4·44	53	5·73	+ 0·04
12	0	10		35	59·87		24	10·13		31	4·39	53	5·74	0·00
	0	20		36	9·86		24	10·14		31	4·36	53	5·78	+ 0·04
	0	30		36	19·89		24	10·11		31	4·33	53	5·78	+ 0·04
12	0	40	4	36	29·96	7	24	10·04	6	31	4·31	53	5·73	− 0·01

13

Telegraphic Signals from Madras to Karachi, 1874, December 13.

Madras Signals.			Karachi Records.			Difference. Kar.—Mad.			Relative Correction.			Karachi West.		Residual Errors.
h.	m.	s.	h.	m.	s.	h.	m.	s.	h.	m.	s.	m.	s.	s.
12	0	50	4	36	39·96	7	24	10·04	6	31	4·28	53	5·76	+ 0·02
	1	10		37	0·01		24	9·99		31	4·23	53	5·76	+ 0·02
	1	20		37	10·06		24	9·94		31	4·20	53	5·74	0·00
	1	30		37	20·08		24	9·92		31	4·17	53	5·75	+ 0·01
	1	40		37	30·11		24	9·89		31	4·15	53	5·74	0·00
	1	50		37	40·37		24	9·63		31	4·12	53	5·51	− 0·23
	2	10		38	0·26		24	9·74		31	4·07	53	5·67	− 0·07
	2	20		38	10·25		24	9·75		31	4·04	53	5·71	− 0·03
	2	30		38	20·17		24	9·83		31	4·01	53	5·82	+ 0·08
	2	40		38	30·23		24	9·77		31	3·98	53	5·79	+ 0·05
	2	50		38	40·23		24	9·77		31	3·96	53	5·81	+ 0·07
	3	10		39	0·38		24	9·62		31	3·90	53	5·72	− 0·02
	3	20		39	10·33		24	9·67		31	3·88	53	5·79	+ 0·05
	3	30		39	20·40		24	9·60		31	3·85	53	5·75	+ 0·01
	3	40		39	30·46		24	9·54		31	3·82	53	5·72	− 0·02
	3	50		39	40·43		24	9·57		31	3·79	53	5·78	+ 0·04
	4	10		40	0·46		24	9·54		31	3·74	53	5·80	+ 0·06
	4	20		40	10·54		24	9·46		31	3·71	53	5·75	+ 0·01
	4	30		40	20·53		24	9·47		31	3·69	53	5·78	+ 0·04
	4	40		40	30·52		24	9·48		31	3·66	53	5·82	+ 0·08
	4	50		40	40·53		24	9·47		31	3·63	53	5·84	+ 0·10
	5	10		41	0·65		24	9·35		31	3·58	53	5·77	+ 0·03
	5	20		41	10·84		24	9·16		31	3·55	53	5·61	− 0·13
	5	30		41	20·72		24	9·28		31	3·52	53	5·76	+ 0·02
	5	40		41	30·81		24	9·19		31	3·50	53	5·09	− 0·05
	5	50		41	40·85		24	9·15		31	3·47	53	5·68	− 0·06
	6	10		42	0·86		24	9·14		31	3·42	53	5·72	− 0·02
	6	20		42	10·88		24	9·12		31	3·39	53	5·73	− 0·01
	6	30		42	20·91		24	9·09		31	3·36	53	5·73	− 0·01
	6	40		42	30·93		24	9·07		31	3·34	53	5·73	− 0·01
	6	50		42	41·00		24	9·00		31	3·31	53	5·09	− 0·05
	7	10		43	1·02		24	8·98		31	3·25	53	5·73	− 0·01
	7	20		43	11·04		24	8·96		31	3·23	53	5·73	− 0·01
	7	30		43	21·00		24	9·00		31	3·20	53	5·80	+ 0·06
	7	40		43	31·18		24	8·82		31	3·17	53	5·65	− 0·09
	7	50		43	41·34		24	8·66		31	3·15	53	5·51	− 0·23
	8	10		44	1·18		24	8·82		31	3·09	53	5·73	− 0·01
12	8	20	4	44	11·23	7	24	8·77	6	31	3·06	53	5·71	− 0·03

Telegraphic Signals from Madras to Karachi, 1874, December 13.

Madras Signals.			Karachi Records.			Difference. Kar.—Mad.			Relative Correction.			Karachi West.		Residual Errors.
h.	m.	s.	h.	m.	s.	h.	m.	s.	h.	m.	s.	m.	s.	s.
12	8	30	4	44	21·26	7	24	8·74	6	31	3·04	53	5·70	− 0·04
	8	40		44	31·24		24	8·76		31	3·01	53	5·75	+ 0·01
	8	50		44	41·31		24	8·69		31	2·98	53	5·71	− 0·03
	9	10		45	1·33		24	8·67		31	2·93	53	5·74	0·00
	9	20		45	11·38		24	8·02		31	2·90	53	5·72	− 0·02
	9	30		45	21·38		24	8·02		31	2·88	53	5·74	0·00
	9	40		45	31·41		24	8·59		31	2·85	53	5·74	0·00
	9	50		45	41·42		24	8·58		31	2·82	53	5·70	+ 0·02
	10	10		46	1·48		24	8·54		31	2·77	53	5·77	+ 0·03
	10	20		46	11·48		24	8·52		31	2·74	53	5·78	+ 0·04
	10	30		46	21·60		24	8·40		31	2·71	53	5·69	− 0·05
	10	40		46	31·56		24	8·44		31	2·69	53	5·75	+ 0·01
	10	50		46	41·56		24	8·44		31	2·66	53	5·78	+ 0·04
	11	10		47	1·58		24	8·42		31	2·61	53	5·81	+ 0·07
	11	20		47	11·73		24	8·27		31	2·58	53	5·69	− 0·05
	11	30		47	21·67		24	8·33		31	2·55	53	5·78	+ 0·04
	11	40		47	31·75		24	8·25		31	2·52	53	5·73	− 0·01
	11	50		47	41·74		24	8·26		31	2·50	53	5·70	+ 0·02
	12	10		48	1·81		24	8·19		31	2·44	53	5·75	+ 0·01
	12	20		48	11·82		24	8·18		31	2·42	53	5·76	+ 0·02
	12	30		48	21·84		24	8·16		31	2·39	53	5·77	+ 0·03
	12	40		48	31·89		24	8·11		31	2·36	53	5·75	+ 0·01
	12	50		48	41·87		24	8·13		31	2·34	53	5·79	+ 0·05
	13	10		49	1·96		24	8·04		31	2·28	53	5·76	+ 0·02
	13	20		49	12·00		24	8·00		31	2·25	53	5·75	+ 0·01
	13	30		49	22·00		24	8·00		31	2·23	53	5·77	+ 0·03
	13	40		49	32·03		24	7·97		31	2·20	53	5·77	+ 0·03
	13	50		49	42·03		24	7·97		31	2·17	53	5·80	+ 0·06
	14	10		50	2·12		24	7·88		31	2·12	53	5·76	+ 0·02
	14	20		50	12·16		24	7·84		31	2·09	53	5·75	+ 0·01
	14	30		50	22·23		24	7·77		31	2·06	53	5·71	− 0·03
	14	40		50	32·21		24	7·79		31	2·04	53	5·75	+ 0·01
12	14	50	4	50	42·24	7	24	7·76	6	31	2·01	53	5·75	+ 0·01
12	5	0·00	4	40	50·66	7	24	9·34	6	31	3·60	53	5·74	0·039

Telegraphic Signals from Karachi to Madras, 1874, December 13.

Madras Records.			Karachi Signals.			Difference. Kar.—Mad.			Relative Correction.			Karachi West.		Residual Errors.
h.	m.	s.	h.	m.	s.	h.	m.	s.	h.	m.	s.	m.	s.	s.
12	24	17·0	5	0	10·43	7	24	6·57	6	31	0·48	53	6·09	+ 0·13
	24	27·0		0	20·42		24	6·58		31	0·45	53	6·13	+ 0·17
	24	36·8		0	30·34		24	6·46		31	0·43	53	6·03	+ 0·07
	24	46·4		0	40·17		24	6·23		31	0·40	53	5·83	− 0·13
	24	57·0		0	50·43		24	6·57	.	31	0·87	53	6·20	+ 0·24
	25	16·0		1	10·42		24	6·48		31	0·32	53	6·16	+ 0·20
	25	26·5		1	20·34		24	6·16		31	0·29	53	5·87	− 0·09
	25	36·5		1	30·19		24	6·31		31	0·27	53	6·04	+ 0·08
	25	46·5		1	40·36		24	6·14		31	0·24	53	5·90	− 0·06
	25	56·4		1	50·33		24	6·07		31	0·21	53	5·86	− 0·10
	26	16·8		2	10·56		24	6·24		31	0·16	53	6·08	+ 0·12
	26	26·3		2	20·33		24	5·97		31	0·13	53	5·84	− 0·12
	26	36·2		2	30·28		24	5·92		31	0·10	53	5·82	− 0·14
	26	46·1		2	40·05		24	6·05		31	0·08	53	5·97	+ 0·01
	26	56·2		2	50·24		24	5·96		31	0·05	53	5·91	− 0·05
	27	16·1		3	10·25		24	5·85		31	0·00	53	5·85	− 0·11
	27	26·1		3	20·25		24	5·85		30	59·97	53	5·88	− 0·08
	27	36·1		3	30·32		24	5·78		30	59·94	53	5·84	− 0·12
	27	46·0		3	40·14		24	5·86		30	59·92	53	5·94	− 0·02
	27	56·0		3	50·18		24	5·82		30	59·89	53	5·93	− 0·03
	28	16·1		4	10·30		24	5·80		30	59·83	53	5·97	+ 0·01
	28	26·0		4	20·29		24	5·71		30	59·81	53	5·90	− 0·06
	28	36·0		4	30·22		24	5·78		30	59·78	53	6·00	+ 0·04
	28	46·1		4	40·32		24	5·78		30	59·75	53	6·03	+ 0·07
	28	56·0		4	50·29		24	5·71		30	59·73	53	5·98	+ 0·02
	29	16·0		5	10·29		24	5·71		30	59·67	53	6·04	+ 0·08
	29	26·0		5	20·34		24	5·66		30	59·65	53	6·01	+ 0·05
	29	36·0		5	30·36		24	5·64		30	59·62	53	6·02	+ 0·06
	29	45·9		5	40·18		24	5·72		30	59·59	53	6·13	+ 0·17
	29	55·9		5	50·30		24	5·60		30	59·56	53	6·04	+ 0·08
	30	16·0		6	10·36		24	5·64		30	59·51	53	6·13	+ 0·17
	30	26·0		6	20·41		24	5·59		30	59·48	53	6·11	+ 0·15
	30	35·8		6	30·34		24	5·46		30	59·46	53	6·00	+ 0·04
	30	45·8		6	40·38		24	5·42		30	59·43	53	5·99	+ 0·03
	30	56·0		6	50·46		24	5·54		30	59·40	53	6·14	+ 0·18
	31	15·6		7	10·28		24	5·32		30	59·35	53	5·97	+ 0·01
	31	25·6		7	20·28		24	5·32		30	59·32	53	6·00	+ 0·04
12	31	35·5	5	7	30·24	7	24	5·26	6	30	59·29	53	5·97	+ 0·01

Telegraphic Signals from Karachi to Madras 1874, December 13.

Madras Records.			Karachi Signals.			Difference. Kar.—Mad.			Relative Correction.			Karachi West.		Residual Errors.
h.	m.	s.	h.	m.	s.	h.	m.	s.	h.	m.	s.	m.	s.	s.
12	31	45·5	5	7	40·28	7	24	5·22	6	30	59·27	53	5·95	− 0·01
	31	55·5		7	50·32		24	5·18		30	·59·24	53	5·94	− 0·02
	32	15·3		8	·10·39		24	4·91		30	59·19	53	5·72	− 0·24
	32	25·5		8	20·58		24	4·92		30	59·16	53	5·76	− 0·20
	32	35·4		8	30·30		24	5·10		30	59·13	53	5·97	+ 0·01
	32	45·3		8	40·22		24	5·08		30	59·11	53	5·97	+ 0·01
	32	55·4		8	50·29		24	5·11		30	59·08	53	6·03	+ 0·07
	33	15·4		9	10·40		24	5·00		30	59·02	53	5·98	+ 0·02
	33	25·3		9	20·46		24	4·84		30	59·00	53	5·84	− 0·12
	33	35·2		9	30·26		24	4·94		30	58·97	53	5·97	+ 0·01
	33	45·2		9	40·44		24	4·76		30	58·94	53	5·82	− 0·14
	33	55·2		9	50·33		24	4·87		30	58·92	53	5·95	− 0·01
	34	15·1		10	10·28		24	4·82		30	58·86	53	5·96	0·00
	34	25·1		10	20·37		24	4·73		30	58·84	53	5·89	− 0·07
	34	35·0		10	30·27		24	4·73		30	58·81	53	5·92	− 0·04
	34	45·0		10	40·26		24	4·74		30	58·78	53	5·96	0·00
	34	55·0		10	50·38		24	4·62		30	58·76	53	5·86	− 0·10
	35	15·0		11	10·31		24	4·69		30	58·70	53	5·99	+ 0·03
	35	25·0		11	20·30		24	4·70		30	58·67	53	6·03	+ 0·07
	35	35·0		11	30·18		24	4·82		30	58·65	53	6·17	+ 0·21
	35	44·8		11	40·20		24	4·60		30	58·62	53	5·98	+ 0·02
	35	55·0		11	50·25		24	4·75		30	58·59	53	6·16	+ 0·20
	36	15·0		12	10·42		24	4·58		30	58·54	53	6·04	+ 0·08
	36	24·5		12	20·21		24	4·29		30	58·51	53	5·78	− 0·18
	36	34·8		12	30·30		24	4·50		30	58·49	53	6·01	+ 0·05
	36	44·7		12	40·23		24	4·47		30	58·46	53	6·01	+ 0·05
	36	54·8		12	50·16		24	4·64		30	58·43	53	6·21	+ 0·25
	37	14·6		13	10·31		24	4·29		30	58·38	53	5·91	− 0·05
	37	24·5		13	20·16		24	4·34		30	58·35	53	5·99	+ 0·03
	37	34·4		13	30·21		24	4·19		30	58·32	53	5·87	− 0·09
	37	44·5		13	40·23		24	4·27		30	58·30	53	5·97	+ 0·01
	37	54·5		13	50·38		24	4·12		30	58·27	53	5·85	− 0·11
	38	14·4		14	10·40		24	4·00		30	58·22	53	5·78	− 0·18
	38	24·2		14	20·25		24	3·95		30	58·19	53	5·76	− 0·20
	38	34·2		14	30·25		24	3·05		30	58·16	53	5·79	− 0·17
	38	44·4		14	40·44		24	3·96		30	58·14	53	5·82	− 0·14
	38	54·4		14	50·48		24	3·92		30	58·11	53	5·81	− 0·15
	39	14·2		15	10·26		24	3·94		30	58·06	53	5·88	− 0·08
	39	24·2		15	20·29		24	3·01		30	58·03	53	5·88	− 0·08
12	39	34·2	5	15	30·34	7	24	3·80	6	30	58·00	53	5·80	− 0·10

14

Telegraphic Signals from Karachi to Madras, 1874, December 13.

Madras Records.			Karachi Signals.			Difference. Kar.—Mad.			Relative Correction.			Karachi West.		Residual Errors.
h.	m.	s.	h.	m.	s.	h.	m.	s.	h.	m.	s.	m.	s.	s.
12	39	44·2	5	15	40·34	7	24	3·86	6	30	57·97	53	5·89	− 0·07
	39	54·1		15	50·16		24	3·94		30	57·95	53	5·99	+ 0·03
	40	14·1		16	10·27		24	3·83		30	57·89	53	5·94	− 0·02
	40	24·1		16	20·10		24	4·00		30	57·87	53	6·13	+ 0·17
	40	34·0		16	30·25		24	3·75		30	57·84	53	5·91	− 0·05
	40	44·0		16	40·27		24	3·73		30	57·81	53	5·92	− 0·04
	40	54·0		16	50·23		24	3·77		30	57·79	53	5·98	+ 0·02
	41	14·0		17	10·33		24	3·67		30	57·73	53	5·94	− 0·02
	41	24·1		17	20·35		24	3·75		30	57·70	53	6·05	+ 0·09
	41	34·0		17	30·32		24	3·68		30	57·68	53	6·00	+ 0·04
	41	43·9		17	40·27		24	3·63		30	57·65	53	5·98	+ 0·02 *.
	41	54·0		17	50·24		24	3·76		30	57·62	53	6·14	+ 0·18
	42	13·9		18	10·29		24	3·61		30	57·57	53	6·04	+ 0·08
	42	23·8		18	20·21		24	3·59		30	57·54	53	6·05	+ 0·09
	42	33·8		18	30·26		24	3·54		30	57·52	53	6·02	+ 0·06
	42	43·6		18	40·22		24	3·38		30	57·49	53	5·89	− 0·07
	42	53·6		18	50·20		24	3·40		30	57·46	53	5·94	− 0·02
	43	13·4		19	10·29		24	3·11		30	57·41	53	5·70	− 0·26
	43	23·5		19	20·27		24	3·23		30	57·38	53	5·85	− 0·11
	43	33·6		19	30·32		24	3·38		30	57·35	53	5·93	− 0·03
	43	43·5		19	40·35		24	3·15		30	57·33	53	5·82	− 0·14
12	43	53·5	5	19	50·19	7	24	3·31	6	30	57·30	53	6·01	+ 0·05
12	34	5·15	5	10	0·30	7	24	4·85	6	30	59·89	53	5·96	0·086

Hence by 100 Telegraphic Signals from Madras, Karachi was West, 53m. 5·74s. ± 0·003s. and by 100 more Signals the reverse way, 53m. 5·90s. ± 0·007s.

Final Results.

	h.	m.	s.
Madras Observatory East of Greenwich	5	20	59·40
General Addison's Station West of Madras	0	53	5·85
G. T. Survey Observatory West of General Addison's...			0·60
G. T. Survey Observatory East of Greenwich.............	4	27	52·95
Probable Error of Signals and Madras Transits...........			± 0·018
Retardation (Current and Instruments.)			0·110

MUDDAPUR.

The determination of the longitude of Muddapur was made at the request of Professor P. Tacchini, Director of the Observatory of Palermo, and also of the "Societa degli Spettroscopisti Italiana", in connection with his observations of the Transit of Venus on December 8th, 1874. Professor Tacchini, being appointed by the Italian Government to superintend an expedition to India, to secure observations, chiefly by the newly discovered spectroscopic method of recording such phenomena, had previously addressed me in regard to the selection of a suitable and conveniently accessible station for the purpose, on the eastern coast, between Madras and Calcutta, at which there would be a probability of fine weather upon the important occasion; but unfortunately I could afford him very little hope of experiencing such in December anywhere near Madras; whereupon he wisely decided upon trying a more northern and inland spot, and selected Muddapur, a station on the East Indian Railway, 183 miles north-west of Calcutta.

A telegram from the Professor, two days after the Transit, announced his more than partial success, although the weather was even there far from favorable. A letter of the same date also reached me from Calcutta, on December 17th, from the Consul General for Italy, the late Monsr. F. Lamouroux; urging co-operation with Professor Tacchini in an early telegraphic longitude determination between Madras and Muddapur. Professor Tacchini's definite proposals and conditional arrangements for carrying out the project followed, under date, Muddapur, December 13th, arriving on the 20th. I replied by telegraph on the 21st, and on Sunday, December 27th, when the telegraph lines could be spared with least inconvenience to the daily traffic on the Government line from Madras to Calcutta, and on the East Indian Railway Company's line from Calcutta to Muddapur, which had to be temporarily joined through for the purpose, the signals were successfully exchanged as detailed in the following pages.

Professor Tacchini's notes of his local time corrections and telegraphic signals were forwarded to me from Calcutta, under date, 1875, January 5th; but I could have wished more details of the former, such as would have enabled me to give the final probable error of the complete operations, instead of having to leave the local time errors indeterminate for Muddapur.

Professor Tacchini, accompanied by Professor Vogel, Dr. Antonio Abetti, and two other gentlemen of the Italian expedition, kindly favored me with a hurried visit on January 23rd, when passing Madras in the French Steamer "Meinam." Preliminary results were duly forwarded to the Professor on May 15th following; differing only from those now given by the slight change, subsequently deduced, in the personal equation of the assistant who observed the star transits at the Madras Observatory.

Madras Sidereal Time Determinations.

Name of Star.	Transit Clock.	Sidereal Correction.	Residual Errors.	Name of Star.	Transit Clock.	Sidereal Corrections.	Residual Errors.
	1874, December 26.				1874, December 28.		
	h. m.	s.	s.		h. m.	s.	s.
Aldebaran......	4 29	− 21·08	− 0·14	α Arietis......	2 1	− 22·44	0·00
ι Aurigæ......	4 40	− 20·93	+ 0·02	67 Ceti.........	2 11	− 22·44	+ 0·01
ε Leporis......	5 1	− 21·08	− 0·12	ξ² Ceti.........	2 22	− 22·37	+ 0·00
Rigel.	5 9	− 20·98	− 0·02	γ Ceti	2 37	− 22·62	− 0·16
β Tauri	5 19	− 20·90	+ 0 07	α Ceti	2 56	− 22·41	+ 0·06
δ Orionis	5 26	− 21·00	− 0·03	δ Arietis......	3 5	− 22·46	+ 0·02
ε Orionis	5 30	− 20·99	− 0·02				
α Columbæ....	5 35	− 20·84	+ 0·14				
Betelgeux.....	5 40	− 21·03	− 0·04				
μ Geminorum	6 16	− 20·90	+ 0·10				
Means..........	5 20	− 20·97	0·070	Means............	2 32	− 22·46	0·055

Mean Sidereal Correction....................1874, December 26, 22h. 17m.................. − 21·53 ± 0·014
Adopted daily change.. − 0·79 ......

Muddapur Mean Time Determinations.

No information afforded as to the way in which the local time was found on by what kind of instrument. Two mean time chronometers were employed, and their corrections being given for noon of each day at Muddapur, it is most probable that solar altitudes were observed.
The following are the corrections communicated by Professor Tacchini.

Chronometer, Whiffin 343.
                           h. m. s.
December 25 ....:........ + 4 50 52·07
  ,,   26........................... + 4 50 48·56
  ,,   27........................ + 4 50 44·94

Chronometer, Dent 1937.
                         h. m. s.
December 26........................... + 5 13 46·50
  ,,   27........................ + 5 13 42·85

Comparisons of Madras Clocks and Chronometer.

Transit Clock.	Sidereal Correction.	Chronometer Carter 337.			Mean Time Correction.	Shepherd's Electrical Clock	Mean Time Correction.
h. m. s.	s.	1874.	h. m. s.		m. s.	h. m. s.	s.
18 8 55	− 21·39	Dec. 26	23 47 35·0		− 1 18·67	......	......
......	......	,, ,, ...	23 57 47·5		− 1 18·67	23 56 30	− 1·17
23 43 20	− 21·58	,, 27	5 21 5·0		− 1 18·64	......	......

Madras and Muddapur Time Corrections, 1874, December 27.

At 0h. 0m. by Shepherd's Electrical Clock, it was 1·17 second fast of Madras Mean Time, with an adopted daily rate of 0·60 second gaining.

At 19h. 9m. by Professor Tacchini's Chronometer, Whiffin 343, it was 4h. 50m. 44·94s. slow of Muddapur Mean Time, with an adopted daily rate of 3·62 seconds gaining.

Hence at 1h. 58m. by Shepherd's Electrical Clock, the relative correction was 4h. 50m. 45·80s. and its change − 0·00210 second per minute.

Telegraphic Signals from Muddapur to Madras, 1874, December 27.

Madras Records.			Muddapur Signals.			Difference. Mad.—Mud.			Relative Correction.			Muddapur East.		Residual Errors.
h.	m.	s.	h.	m.	s.	h.	m.	s.	h.	m.	s.	m.	s.	s.
1	53	23·9	21	28	0	4	25	23·9	4	50	45·81	25	21·91	+ 0·09
	53	33·8		28	10		25	23·8		50	45·81	25	22·01	+ 0·19
	53	44·0		28	20		25	24·0		50	45·81	25	21·81	− 0·01
	53	53·9		28	30		25	23·9		50	45·81	25	21·91	+ 0·09
	54	3·8		28	40		25	23·8		50	45·81	25	22·01	+ 0·19
	54	14·0		28	50		25	24·0		50	45·81	25	21·81	− 0·01
	54	24·0		29	0		25	24·0		50	45·81	25	21·81	− 0·01
	54	44·0		29	20		25	24·0		50	45·81	25	21·81	−·0·01
	54	53·9		29	30		25	23·9		50	45·81	25	21·91	+ 0·09
2	1	34·0		36	10		25	24·0		50	45·79	25	21·79	− 0·03
	1	44·0		36	20		25	24·0		50	45·79	25	21·79	− 0·03
	1	53·9		36	30		25	23·9		50	45·79	25	21·89	+ 0·07
	2	4·0		36	40		25	24·0		50	45·79	25	21·79	− 0·03
	2	14·0		36	50		25	24·0		50	45·79	25	21·79	− 0·03
	2	24·0		37	0		25	24·0		50	45·79	25	21·79	− 0·03
	2	34·0		37	10		25	24·0		50	45·79	25	21·79	− 0·03
	2	44·0		37	20		25	24·0		50	45·79	25	21·70	− 0·03
	2	54·0		37	30		25	24·0		50	45·79	25	21·79	− 0·03
	3	4·0		37	40		25	24·0		50	45·79	25	21·79	− 0·03
	3	14·0		37	50		25	24·0		50	45·79	25	21·79	− 0·03
	3	24·0		38	0		25	24·0		50	45·79	25	21·79	− 0·03
	3	33·9		38	10		25	23·9		50	45·79	25	21·89	+ 0·07
	3	43·9		38	20		25	23·9		50	45·79	25	21·89	+ 0·07
	3	54·0		38	30		25	24·0		50	45·79	25	21·79	− 0·03
	4	4·0		38	40		25	24·0		50	45·79	25	21·79	− 0·03
	4	14·0		38	50		25	24·0		50	45·79	25	21·79	− 0·03
	4	24·0		39	0		25	24·0		50	45·79	25	21·79	− 0·03
2	4	33·9	21	39	10	4	25	23·9	4	50	45·79	25	21·89	+ 0·07

15

Telegraphic Signals from Muddapur to Madras, 1874, December 27.

Madras Records.			Muddapur Signals.			Difference. Mad.—Mud.			Relative Correction.			Muddapur East.			Residual Errors.
h.	m.	s.	h.	m.	s.	h.	m.	s.	h.	m.	s.		m.	s.	s.
2	4	43·8	21	39	20	4	25	23·8	4	50	45·79		25	21·99	+ 0·17
	4	54·0		39	30		25	24·0		50	45·79		25	21·79	− 0·03
	5	4·0		39	40		25	24·0		50	45·79		25	21·79	− 0·03
	5	14·0		39	50		25	24·0		50	45·78		25	21·78	− 0·04
	5	23·8		40	0		25	23·8		50	45·78		25	21·98	+ 0·16
	5	34·0		40	10		25	24·0		50	45·78		25	21·78	− 0·04
	5	43·9		40	20		25	23·9		50	45·78		25	21·88	+ 0·06
	6	3·8		40	40		25	23·8		50	45·78		25	21·98	+ 0·16
	6	14·0		40	50		25	24·0		50	45·78		25	21·78	− 0·04
	6	24·0		41	0		25	24·0		50	45·78		25	21·78	− 0·04
	6	34·0		41	10		25	24·0		50	45·78		25	21·78	− 0·04
	6	44·0		41	20		25	24·0		50	45·78		25	21·78	− 0·04
	6	53·9		41	30		55	23·9		50	45·78		25	21·88	+ 0·06
	7	3·9		41	40		25	23·9		50	45·78		25	21·88	+ 0·06
	7	14·0		41	50		25	24·0		50	45·78		25	21·78	− 0·04
	7	24·0		42	0		25	24·0		50	45·78		25	21·78	− 0·04
	7	34·0		42	10		25	24·0		50	45·78		25	21·78	− 0·04
	7	44·0		42	20		25	24·0		50	45·78		25	21·78	− 0·04
	7	54·0		42	30		25	24·0		50	45·78		25	21·78	− 0·04
	8	3·9		42	40		25	23·9		50	45·78		25	21·88	+ 0·06
	8	13·9		42	50		25	23·9		50	45·78		25	21·88	+ 0·06
	8	24·0		43	0		25	24·0		50	45·78		25	21·76	− 0·04
	8	34·0		43	10		25	24·0		50	45·78		25	21·78	− 0·04
	8	44·0		43	20		25	24·0		50	45·78		25	21·78	− 0·04
	9	3·8		43	40		25	23·8		50	45·78		25	21·98	+ 0·16
	9	14·0		43	50		25	24·0		50	45·78		25	21·78	− 0·04
	9	24·0		44	0		25	24·0		50	45·78		25	21·78	− 0·04
	9	34·1		44	10		25	24·1		50	45·78		25	21·68	− 0·14
	9	44·0		44	20		25	24·0		50	45·78		25	21·78	− 0·04
	9	54·0		44	30		25	24·0		50	45·78		25	21·78	− 0·04
	10	3·8		44	40		25	23·8		50	45·77		25	21·97	+ 0·15
	10	14·0		44	50		25	24·0		50	45·77		25	21·77	− 0·05
	10	34·0		45	10		25	24·0		50	45·77		25	21·77	− 0·05
	10	44·0		45	20		25	24·0		50	45·77		25	21·77	− 0·05
	10	54·1		45	30		25	24·1		50	45·77		25	21·67	− 0·15
	11	4·0		45	40		25	24·0		50	45·77		25	21·77	− 0·05
	11	14·0		45	50		25	24·0		50	45·77		25	21·77	− 0·05
	11	44·0		46	20		25	24·0		50	45·77		25	21·77	− 0·05
	11	54·0		46	30		25	24·0		50	45·77		25	21·77	− 0·05
2	12	4·0	21	46	40	4	25	24·0	4	50	45·77		25	21·77	− 0·05

Telegraphic Signals from Muddapur to Madras, 1874, December 27.

Madras Records.			Muddapur Signals.			Difference. Mad.—Mud.			Relative Correction.			Muddapur East.		Residual Errors.
h.	m.	s.	h.	m.	s.	h.	m.	s.	h.	m.	s.	m.	s.	s.
2	12	14·0	21	46	50	4	25	24·0	4	50	45·77	25	21·77	− 0·05
	12	24·0		47	0		25	24·0		50	45·77	25	21·77	− 0·05
2	5	8·25	21	39	44·20	4	25	23·96	4	50	45·78	25	21·82	0·058

Telegraphic Signals from Madras to Muddapur, 1874, December 27.

Madras Signals.			Muddapur Records.			Difference. Mad.—Mud.			Relative Correction.			Muddapur East.		Residual Errors.
h.	m.	s.	h.	m.	s.	h.	m.	s.	h.	m.	s.	m.	s.	s.
2	20	0	21	54	36·3	4	25	23·7	4	50	45·75	25	22·05	+ 0·13
	20	10		54	46·2		25	23·8		50	45·75	25	21·95	+ 0·03
	20	20		54	56·4		25	23·6		50	45·75	25	22·15	+ 0·23
	20	30		55	6·2		25	23·8		50	45·75	25	21·95	+ 0·03
	20	40		55	16·2		25	23·8		50	45·75	25	21·05	+ 0·03
	20	50		55	26·1		25	23·0		50	45·75	25	21·85	− 0·07
	21	0		55	36·2		25	23·8		50	45·75	25	21·95	+ 0·03
	21	10		55	46·1		25	23·9		50	45·75	25	21·85	− 0·07
	21	20		55	56·1		25	23·9		50	45·75	25	21·85	− 0·07
	21	30		56	6·2		25	23·8		50	45·75	25	21·95	+ 0·03
	21	40		56	16·0		25	24·0		50	45·75	25	21·75	− 0·17
	21	50		56	26·3		25	23·7		50	45·75	25	22·05	+ 0·13
	22	0		56	36·3		25	23·7		50	45·75	25	22·05	+ 0·13
	22	10		56	46·1		25	23·9		50	45·75	25	21·85	− 0·07
	22	20		56	56·1		25	23·9		50	45·75	25	21·85	− 0·07
	22	30		57	6·4		25	23·0		50	45·75	25	22·15	+ 0·23
	22	40		57	16·1		25	23·0		50	45·75	25	21·85	− 0·07
	22	50		57	26·0		25	24·0		50	45·75	25	21·75	− 0·17
	23	0		57	36·3		25	23·7		50	45·75	25	22·05	+ 0·13
	23	10		57	46·3		25	23·7		50	45·75	25	22·05	+ 0·13
	23	20		57	56·2		25	23·8		50	45·75	25	21·95	+ 0·03
	23	30		58	6·4		25	23·6		50	45·75	25	22·15	+ 0·23
	23	40		58	16·1		25	23·9		50	45·75	25	21·85	− 0·07
	23	50		58	26·3		25	23·7		50	45·75	25	22·05	+ 0·13
2	24	0	21	58	36·1	4	25	23·9	4	50	45·75	25	21·85	− 0·07

Telegraphic Signals from Madras to Muddapur, 1874, December 27.

Madras Signals.			Muddapur Records.			Difference. Mad.—Mud.			Relative Correction.			Muddapur East.		Residual Errors.
h.	*m.*	*s.*	*h.*	*m.*	*s.*	*h.*	*m.*	*s.*	*h.*	*m.*	*s.*	*m.*	*s.*	*s.*
2	24	10	21	58	46·2	4	25	23·8	4	50	45·75	25	21·05	+ 0·03
	24	20		58	56·4		25	23·6		50	45·74	25	22·14	+ 0·22
	24	30		59	6·2		25	23·8		50	45·74	25	21·94	+ 0·02
	24	40		59	16·0		25	24·0		50	45·74	25	21·74	− 0·18
	24	50		59	26·2		25	23·8		50	45·74	25	21·94	+ 0·02
	25	0		59	36·1		25	23·9		50	45·74	25	21·84	− 0·08
	25	10		59	46·1		25	23·9		50	45·74	25	21·84	− 0·08
	25	20		59	56·2		25	23·8		50	45·74	25	21·94	+ 0·02
	25	30	22	0	6·1		25	23·9		50	45·74	25	21·84	− 0·08
	25	40		0	16·2		25	23·8		50	45·74	25	21·94	+ 0·02
	25	50		0	26·0		25	24·0		50	45·74	25	21·74	− 0·16
	26	0		0	36·1		25	23·9		50	45·74	25	21·84	− 0·08
	26	10		0	46·2		25	23·8		50	45·74	25	21·94	+ 0·02
	26	20		0	56·3		25	23·7		50	45·74	25	22·04	+ 0·12
	26	30		1	6·3		25	23·7		50	45·74	25	22·04	+ 0·12
	26	40		1	16·3		25	23·7		50	45·74	25	22·04	+ 0·12
	26	50		1	26·2		25	23·8		50	45·74	25	21·94	+ 0·02
	27	0		1	36·1		25	23·9		50	45·74	25	21·84	− 0·08
	27	10		1	46·2		25	23·8		50	45·74	25	21·94	+ 0·02
	27	20		1	56·2		25	23·8		50	45·74	25	21·94	+ 0·02
	27	30		2	6·1		25	23·9		50	45·74	25	21·84	− 0·08
	27	40		2	16·1		25	23·9		50	45·74	25	21·84	− 0·08
	28	0		2	36·1		25	23·9		50	45·74	25	21·84	− 0·08
	28	10		2	46·2		25	23·8		50	45·74	25	21·94	+ 0·02
	28	20		2	56·2		25	23·8		50	45·74	25	21·94	+ 0·02
	28	30		3	6·3		25	23·7		50	45·74	25	22·04	+ 0·12
	28	40		3	16·3		25	23·7		50	45·74	25	22·04	+ 0·12
	28	50		3	26·0		25	24·0		50	45·74	25	21·74	− 0·18
	29	0		3	36·1		25	23·9		50	45·73	25	21·83	− 0·09
	29	10		3	46·2		25	23·8		50	45·73	25	21·93	+ 0·01
	29	20		3	56·3		25	23·7		50	45·73	25	22·03	+ 0·11
	29	30		4	6·3		25	23·7		50	45·73	25	22·03	+ 0·11
	29	40		4	16·1		25	23·9		50	45·73	25	21·83	− 0·09
	29	50		4	26·0		25	24·0		50	45·73	25	21·73	− 0·19
2	30	0	22	4	36·1	4	25	23·9	4	50	45·73	25	21·83	− 0·09
2	24	57·17	21	59	33·35	4	25	23·82	4	50	45·74	25	21·92	0·091

Madras and Muddapur Time Correctons, 1874, December 27.

At 0h. 0m. by Shephord's Electrical Clock it was 1·17 second fast of Madras Mean Time, with an adopted daily rate of 0·60 second gaining.

At 19h. 46m. by Professor Tacchini's Chronometer Dent 1937, it was 5h. 13m. 42·85s. slow of Muddapur Mean Time, with an adopted daily rate of 3·74 seconds gaining.

Hence at 2h. 48m. by Shepherd's Electrical Clock, the Relative Correction was 5h. 13m. 43·59s. and its change — 0·00218 second per minute.

Telegraphic Signals from Muddapur to Madras, 1874, December 27. .

Madras Records.			Muddapur Signals.			Difference. Mad.—Mud.			Relative Correction.			Muddapur East.		Residual Errors.
h.	m.	s.	h.	m.	s.	h.	m.	s.	h.	m.	s.	m.	s.	s.
2	37	31·1	21	49	10	4	48	21·1	5	13	43·61	25	22·51	+ 0·33
	37	41·2		49	20		48	21·2		13	43·61	25	22·41	+ 0·23
	37	51·4		49	30		48	21·4		13	43·61	25	22·21	+ 0·03
	38	1·4		49	40		48	21·4		13	43·61	25	22·21	+ 0·03
	38	21·3		50	0		48	21·3		13	43·61	25	22·31	+ 0·13
	38	31·5		50	10		48	21·5		13	43·61	25	22·11	− 0·07
	38	51·5		50	30		48	21·5		13	43·61	25	22·11	− 0·07
	43	21·2		55	0		48	21·2		13	43·60	25	22·40	+ 0·22
	43	31·2		55	10		48	21·2		13	43·60	25	22·40	+ 0·22
	43	41·3		55	20		48	21·3		13	43·60	25	22·30	+ 0·12
	43	51·2		55	30	.	48	21·2		13	43·60	25	22·40	+ 0·22
	44	1·4		55	40		48	21·4		13	43·60	25	22·20	+ 0·02
	44	11·2		55	50		48	21·2		13	43·60	. 25	22·40	+ 0·22
	44	21·5		56	0		48	21·5		13	43·60	25	22·10	− 0·08
	44	31·5		56	10		48	21·5		13	43·60	25	22·10	− 0·08
	44	41·2		56	20		48	21·2		13	43·60	25	22·40	+ 0·22
	44	51·3		56	30		48	21·3		13	43·60	25	22·30	+ 0·12
	45	1·2		56	40		48	21·2		13	43·60	25	22·40	+ 0·22
	45	11·1		56	50		48	21·1		13	43·60	25	22·50	+ 0·32
	45	21·1		57	0		48	21·1		13	43·60	25	22·50	+ 0·32
	45	31·3		57	10		48	21·3		13	43·60	25	22·30	+ 0·12
	45	41·3		57	20		48	21·3		13	43·60	25	22·30	+ 0·12
	45	51·4		57	30		48	21·4		13	43·59	25	22·19	+ 0·01
	46	1·2		57	40		48	21·2		13	43·59	25	22·39	+ 0·21
2	46	11·2	21	57	50	4	48	21·2	5	13	43·59	25	22·39	+ 0·21

Telegraphic Signals from Muddapur to Madras, 1874, December 27.

Madras Records.			Muddapur Signals.			Difference. Mad.—Mud.			Relative Correction.			Muddapur East.		Residual Errors.
h.	m.	s.	h.	m.	s.	h.	m.	s.	h.	m.	s.	m.	s.	s.
2	46	21·4	21	58	0	4	48	21·4	5	13	43·59	25	22·19	+ 0·01
	46	31·4		58	10		48	21·4		13	43·59	25	22·19	+ 0·01
	46	41·6		58	20		48	21·6		13	43·59	25	21·99	− 0·19
	46	51·6		58	30		48	21·6		13	43·59	25	21·99	− 0·19
	47	1·2		58	40		48	21·2		13	43·59	25	22·39	+ 0·21
	47	11·2		58	50		48	21·2		13	43·59	25	22·39	+ 0·21
	47	21·4		·59	0		48	21·4		13	43·59	25	22·19	+ 0·01
	47·	31·5		59	10		48	21·5		13	43·59	25	22·00	− 0·09
	47	41·7		59	20		48	21·7		13	43·59	25	21·80	− 0·29
	47	51·6		59	30		48	21·6		13	43·59	25	21·90	− 0·19
	48	1·6		59	40		48	21·6		13	43·59	25	21·99	− 0·1b·
	48	21·6	22	0	0		48	21·6		13	43·59	25	21·90	− 0·19
	48	31·6		0	10		48	21·6		13	43·59	25	21·99	− 0·19
	48	41·6		0	20		48	21·6		13	43·59	25	21·90	− 0·19
	48	51·7		0	30		48	21·7		13	43·59	25	21·89	− 0·29
	49	1·8		0	40		48	21·8		13	43·59	25	21·79	− 0·39
	49	11·6		0	50		48	21·6		13	43·59	25	21·99	− 0·19
	40	21·4		1	0		48	21·4		13	43·59	25	22·19	+ 0·01
	49	31·5		1	10		48	21·5		13	43·59	25	22·00	− 0·09
	49	41·6		1	20		48	21·6		13	43·59	25	21·90	− 0·19
	40	51·6		1	30		48	21·6		13	43·59	25	21·90	− 0·19
	50	1·7		1	40		48	21·7		13	43·59	25	21·89	− 0·29
	50	11·5		1	50		48	21·5		13	43·59	25	22·09	− 0·00
	50	21·4		2	0		48	21·4		13	43·58	25	22·18	0·00
	50	31·5		2	10		48	21·5		13	43·58	25	22·08	− 0·10
	50	41·3		2	20		48	21·3		13	43·58	25	22·28	+ 0·10
	50	51·5		2	30		48	21·5		13	43·58	25	22·08	− 0·10
	51	1·5		2	40		48	21·5		13	43·58	25	22·08	− 0·10
	51	11·4		2	50		48	21·4		13	43·58	25	22·18	0·00
	51	21·2		3	0		48	21·2		13	43·58	25	22·38	+ 0·20
	51	31·4		3	10		48	21·4		13	43·58	25	22·18	0·00
	51	41·2		3	20		48	21·2		13	43·58	25	22·38	+ 0·20
	52	1·2		3	40		48	21·2		13	43·58	25	22·38	+ 0·20
	52	11·6		3	50		48	21·6		13	43·58	25	21·08	− 0·20
	52	21·2		4	0		48	21·2		13	43·58	25	22·38	+ 0·20
	52	31·5		4	10		48	21·5		13	43·58	25	22·08	− 0·10
	52	41·4		4	20		48	21·4		13	43·58	25	22·18	0·00
	52	51·5		4	30		48	21·5		13	43·58	25	22·08	− 0·10
2	53	1·5	22	4	40	4	48	21·5	5	13	43·58	25	22·08	− 0·10

Telegraphic Signals from Muddapur to Madras, 1874, December 27.

Madras Records.	Muddapur Signals.	Difference. Mad.—Mud.	Relative Correction.	Muddapor East.	Residual Errors.
h. m. s.	h. m. s.	h. m. s.	h. m. s.	m. s.	s.
2 53 11·5	22 4 50	4 48 21·5	5 13 43·58	25 22·08	− 0·10
53 21·5	5 0	48 21·5	13 43·58	25 22·08	− 0·10
2 47 13·23	21 58 51·82	4 48 21·41	5 13 43·59	25 22·18	0·148

Telegraphic Signals from Madras to Muddapur, 1874, December 27.

Madras Signals.	Muddapur Records.	Difference. Mad.− Mud.	Relative Correction.	Muddapur East.	Residual Errors.
h. m. s.	h. m. s.	h. m. s.	h. m. s.	m. s.	s.
3 0 10	22 11 48·8	4 48 21·2	5 13 43·56	25 22·36	− 0·05
0 20	11 58·8	48 21·2	13 43·56	25 22·36	− 0·05
0 30	12 8·9	48 21·1	13 43·56	25 22·46	+ 0·05
0 40	12 18·8	48 21·2	13 43·56	25 22·36	− 0·05
0 50	12 29·1	48 20·9	13 43·56	25 22·66	+ 0·25
1 0	12 38·8	48 21·2	13 43·56	25 22·36	− 0·05
1 10	12 49·0	48 21·0	13 43·56	25 22·56	+ 0·15
1 20	12 59·1	48 20·9	13 43·56	25 22·66	+ 0·25
1 30	13 8·9	48 21·1	13 43·56	25 22·46	+ 0·05
1 40	13 19·0	48 21·0	13 43·56	25 22·56	+ 0·15
1 50	13 28·9	48 21·1	13 43·56	25 22·46	+ 0·05
2 0	13 39·0	48 21·0	13 43·56	25 22·56	+ 0·15
2 10	13 49·0	48 21·0	13 43·56	25 22·56	+ 0·15
2 20	13 58·9	48 21·1	13 43·56	25 22·46	+ 0·05
2 30	14 9·2	48 20·8	13 43·56	25 22·76	+ 0·35
2 40	14 18·8	48 21·2	13 43·56	25 22·36	− 0·05
2 50	14 28·9	48 21·1	13 43·56	25 22·46	+ 0·05
3 0	14 39·0	48 21·0	13 43·56	25 22·56	+ 0·15
3 10	14 48·9	48 21·1	13 43·56	25 22·46	+ 0·05
3 20	14 58·9	48 21·1	13 43·56	25 22·46	+ 0·05
3 30	15 8·8	48 21·2	13 43·56	25 22·36	− 0·05
3 40	15 18·8	48 21·2	13 43·56	25 22·36	− 0·05
3 50	15 28·8	48 21·2	13 43·56	25 22·36	− 0·05
4 0	15 39·1	48 20·9	13 43·56	25 22·66	+ 0·25
4 10	15 49·1	48 20·9	13 43·55	25 22·65	+ 0·24
3 4 20	22 15 59·1	4 48 20·9	5 13 43·55	25 22·65	+ 0·24

Telegraphic Signals from Madras to Muddapur, 1874, December 27.

Madras Signals.			Muddapur Records.			Difference. Mad.—Mud.			Relative Correction.			Muddapur West.			Residual Errors.
h.	m.	s.	h.	m.	s.	h.	m.	s.	h.	m.	s.		m.	s.	s.
3	4	30	22	16	9·0	4	48	21·0	5	13	43·55		25	22·55	+ 0·14
	4	40		16	19·1		48	20·9		13	43·55		25	22·65	+ 0·24
	4	50		16	29·0		48	21·0		13	43·55		25	22·55	+ 0·14
	5	0		16	38·0		48	21·1		13	43·55		25	22·45	+ 0·04
	5	10		16	48·0		48	21·1		13	43·55		25	22·45	+ 0·04
	5	20		16	59·1		48	20·9		13	43·55		25	22·65	+ 0·24
	5	30		17	8·7		48	21·3		13	43·55		25	22·25	− 0·16
	5	40		17	19·1		48	20·9		13	43·55		25	22·65	+ 0·24
	5	50		17	28·0		48	21·1		13	43·55		25	22·45	+ 0·04
	6	0		17	38·0		48	21·1		13	43·55		25	22·45	+ 0·04
	6	10		17	48·8		48	21·2		13	43·55		25	22·35	− 0·06
	6	20		17	58·8		48	21·2		13	43·55		25	22·35	− 0·06
	6	30		18	8·7		48	21·3		13	43·55		25	22·25	− 0·16
	6	40		18	18·8		48	21·2		13	43·55		25	22·35	− 0·06
	6	50		18	28·6		48	21·4		13	43·55		25	22·15	− 0·26
	7	0		18	38·6		48	21·4		13	43·55		25	22·15	− 0·26
	7	10		18	48·7		48	21·3		13	43·55		25	22·25	− 0·16
	7	20		18	58·7		48	21·3		13	43·55		25	22·25	− 0·16
	7	30		19	8·6		48	21·4		13	43·55		25	22·15	− 0·26
	7	40		19	18·7		48	21·3		13	43·55		25	22·25	− 0·16
	7	50		19	28·7		48	21·3		13	43·55		25	22·25	− 0·16
	8	0		19	38·7		48	21·3		13	43·55		25	22·25	− 0·16
	8	10		19	48·7		48	21·3		13	43·55		25	22·25	− 0·16
	8	20		19	58·0		48	21·1		13	43·55		25	22·45	+ 0·04
	8	30		20	8·9		48	21·1		13	43·55		25	22·45	+ 0·04
	8	40		20	18·8		48	21·2		13	43·54		25	22·34	− 0·07
	8	50		20	28·6		48	21·2		13	43·54		25	22·34	− 0·07
	9	0		20	38·7		48	21·3		13	43·54		25	22·24	− 0·17
	9	10		20	48·7		48	21·3		13	43·54		25	22·24	− 0·17
	9	20		20	58·9		48	21·1		13	43·54		25	22·44	+ 0·03
	9	30		21	8·8		48	21·2		13	43·54		25	22·34	− 0·07
	9	40		21	18·7		48	21·3		13	43·54		25	22·24	− 0·17
	9	50		21	28·7		48	21·3		13	43·54		25	22·24	− 0·17
3	10	0	22	21	38·7	4	48	21·3	5	13	43·54		25	22·24	− 0·17
3	5	5·00	22	16	43·86	4	48	21·14	5	13	43·55		25	22·41	0·127

Summary of Telegraphic Results.

Number of Signals.			Muddapur East.	Probable Errors.	Compound Retardation.
			m. *s.*	*s.*	*s.*
By 70 from Muddapur	...	...	25 21·82	± 0·006	0·050
By 60 from Madras		...	25 21·92	± 0·010	
By 66 from Muddapur		...	25 22·18	± 0·015	0·115
By 60 from Madras	...	... ...	25 22·41	± 0·014	

Final Results.

	h.	*m.*	*s.*
Madras Observatory East of Greenwich.	5	20	59·40
Muddapur East of Madras.		25	22·08
Muddapur East of Greenwich.	5	46	21·48
Probable Error of Signals and Madras Transits ...			± 0·018
Compound Retardation. (Current and Instruments.)...			0·082

ROOKKEE.

The last telegraphic determination called for was also required in connection with the Transit of Venus, in December, 1874. Lieut. Col. J. F. Tennant, R. E., having secured successful observations of the Transit at Roorkee, desired my co-operation in settling his longitude by means of telegraphic signals soon after the event as usual, and was promised all needful aid therein. To my surprise and regret however, as the time for carrying out the work approached, I discovered that Col. Tennant's idea of co-operation differed so widely from mine that there seemed little chance of the work being accomplished at all. After much needless delay, a better understanding was arrived at through the mediation of our esteemed mutual friend, Captain W. M. Campbell, R. E., and the necessary telegraphic signals were satisfactorily exchanged on three nights, viz., on May 31st, June 2nd and 5th.

The signals and records at Madras were given and made by me, as on the last two occasions, by Shepherd's Electrical Clock, the standard of mean time for all India; and by Colonel Tennant, at Roorkee, with his Sidereal Transit Clock. A further check upon the work was however independently obtained on the first two evenings, by Captain Campbell making separate notes of my first series of taps to Roorkee and of Colonel Tennant's first series therefrom. A third check was also secured on all three nights, by the record of Col. Tennant's second series of signals from Roorkee upon the Madras Chronograph, thanks to Captain Campbell's valuable and obliging assistance in the working of the instrument while I was otherwise engaged.

As Captain Campbell, when reading the times of my taps to Roorkee, only differed 0·1 second from me in one out of the thirty-six signals he recorded, and as the fifty-seven Madras signals compared with the fifty-four from Roorkee, marked on the Madras Chronograph, have been given in detail, I have not thought it necessary to print the times of each separate signal in the two checks, but have shewn the mean results of each series, given and received, for comparison with the similar results of my own records, which were made by eye and ear throughout. It will be seen that Captain Campbell's independent records, by eye and ear, gave a final longitude of Roorkee only 0·03 second greater than my own, while the chronographic process yielded a result 0·05 second less.

Advantage was taken of Captain Campbell's presence, to compare his personal equation for star transits, relatively to my own and those of the native assistants who made most of the transit observations for finding the Madras time corrections. From these comparisons it followed, that, had his time observations been used instead of mine, the resulting longitude would have been 0·35 second less than that I have adopted.

Sidereal Time Determinations.

MADRAS.				ROORKEE.
1875, May 31.				1875, May 31.
Star.	Transit Clock.	Sidereal Correction.	Residual Errors.	
	h. m.	s.	s.	
θ Virginis.........	13 3	+ 17·23	− 0·03	
3 Virginis.....	13 28	+ 17·25	− 0·02	
η Bootis.........	13 48	+ 17·24	− 0·03	
τ Virginis.,.....	13 55	+ 17·16	− 0·11	Roorkee sidereal time was determined by Lieut.-Col. Tennant, by means of a transit instrument, an
ρ Bootis.........	14 26	+ 17·36	+ 0·09	electrical clock and a chronograph. No details were however furnished, not even as to the number of
3 Ophiuchi....	16 8	+ 17·27	− 0·02	stars upon which the result depended.
Antares.........	16 21	+ 17·28	− 0·01	At 15h. 27m. by the transit clock its correction was
3 Herculis.....	16 36	+ 17·43	+ 0·14	stated to be + 6·83 seconds and its daily change
κ Ophiuchi....	16 51	+ 17·27	− 0·02	− .2·40 seconds.
α Herculis.....	17 9	+ 17·33	+ 0·03	
Means.........	15 11	+ 17·28	0·050	

Probable error of mean correction .... ± 0·014

Adopted daily change............................ + 0·19

Sidereal Time Determinations.

MADRAS.				ROORKEE.
1875, June 2.				**1875, June 2.**

Star.	Transit Clock.	Sidereal Correction.	Residual Errors.
	h. m.	s.	s.
β Corvi.......	12 28	+ 17·32	− 0·14
θ Virginis.....	13 3	+ 17·43	− 0·02
Spica...........	13 18	+ 17·47	+ 0·02
3 Virginis	13 28	+ 17·47	+ 0·02
η Bootis	13 48	+ 17·42	− 0·04
τ Virginis	13 55	+ 17·46	0·00
Arcturus......	14 10	+ 17·54	+ 0·08
ρ Bootis........	14 26	+ 17·56	+ 0·10
3 Herculis.....	16 36	+ 17·58	+ 0·10
θ Ophiuchi.....	17 14	+ 17·33	− 0·16
Means	14 15	+ 17·46	0·068

At 15h. 38·5m. by Roorkee transit clock its correction was stated to be + 3·67 seconds and its daily change + 0·60 second.

Probable error of mean correction...... ± 0·019

Adopted daily change............................. + 0·23

1875, June 5.				**1875, June 5.**

β Corvi........	12 28	+ 18·10	− 0·01
Spica	13 18	+ 18·05	− 0·06
η Bootis........	13 48	+ 18·01	− 0·11
τ Virginis......	13 55	+ 18·10	− 0·02
Arcturus.......	14 10	+ 18·13	+ 0·01
ρ Bootis........	14 26	+ 18·21	+ 0·09
ε Bootis........	14 39	+ 18·25	+ 0·13

MADRAS.				ROORKEE.
1875, June 5—*continued.*				1875, June 5—*continued.*

Star.	Transit Clock.	Sidereal Correction.	Residual Errors.
	h. m.	s.	s.
a³ Libræ......	14 44	+ 18·10	− 0·02
ψ Bootis.......	14 59	+ 18·21	+ 0·09
β¹ Scorpii.....	15 58	− 18·05	− 0·08
Means..........	14 15	+ 18·12	0·062

At 15h. 49·2m. by Roorkee transit clock, its correction was stated to have been + 5·18 seconds and its daily change + 1·00 second.

Probable error of mean correction ...   ± 0·017

Adopted daily change ...   .   + 0·14

Comparisons of Madras Clocks and Chronometer.

Transit Clock.	Sidereal Correction.	Chronometer Carter 703.			Mean Time Correction.	Shepherd's ElectricalClock.	Mean Time Correction.
h. m. s.	s.	1874. h. m. s.			s.	h. m. s.	s.
16 54 53	+ 17·29	May 31... 12 20 10·0			− 26·91	......	......
		„ „... 12 33 26·5			− 26·85	12 33 0	− 0·35
......	......	„ „... 16 10 26·0			− 25·94	16 10 0	+ 0·06
20 53 6	+ 17·32	„ „... 16 17 43·0			− 25·91		
16 47 12	+ 17·48	June 2 ... 12 4 27·0			− 15·29	......	......
......	......	„ „... 12 10 14·5			− 15·26	12 10 0	− 0·76
......	......	„ „... 14 18 14·0			− 14·70	14 18 0	− 0·70
19 10 2	+ 17·51	„ „... 14 26 53·0			− 14·66	......	......
16 23 49	+ 18·13	„ 5 ... 11 29 3·0			+ 2·45	......	......
		„ „... 11 33 56·5			+ 2·47	11 34 0	− 1·03
......	......	„ „... 15 54 55·5			+ 3·42	15 55 0	− 1·08
21 4 37	+ 18·16	„ „... 16 9 4·0			+ 3·47	......	......

Madras and Roorkee Time Corrections, 1875, May 31.

At 12*h*. 33*m*. by Shepherd's Electrical Clock, it was 0·35 second fast of Madras Mean Time, with an adopted daily rate of 2·72 seconds losing.

At 15*h*. 27*m*. by Lieut. Col. Tennant's Transit Clock, it was 6·83 seconds slow of Roorkee Sidereal Time, with an adopted daily rate of 2·40 seconds gaining.

Hence at 12*h*. 47*m*. by Shepherd's Electrical Clock, the Relative Correction was 4*h*. 35*m*. 24·72*s*. and its change + 0·16783 second per minute.

Telegraphic Signals from Madras to Roorkee, 1875, May 31.

Madras Signals.			Roorkee Records.			Difference. Roor.—Mad.			Relative Correction.			Roorkee West.		Residual Errors.
h.	m.	s.	h.	m.	s.	h.	m.	s.	h.	m.	s.	m.	s.	s.
12	47	0	17	12	58·38	4	25	58·38	4	35	24·72	9	26·34	+ 0·04
	47	10		13	8·44		25	58·44		35	24·75	9	26·31	+ 0·01
	47	20		13	18·43		25	58·43		35	24·78	9	26·35	+ 0·04
	47	30		13	28·50		25	58·50		35	24·80	9	26·30	0·00
	47	40		13	38·51		25	58·51		35	24·83	9	26·32	+ 0·02
	47	50		13	48·50		25	58·50		35	24·86	9	26·36	+ 0·06
	48	0		13	58·53		25	58·53		35	24·89	9	26·36	+ 0·06
	48	10		14	8·55		25	58·55		35	24·92	9	26·37	+ 0·07
	48	20		14	18·58		25	58·58		35	24·94	9	26·36	+ 0·06
	48	30		14	28·73		25	58·73		35	24·97	9	26·24	− 0·06
	48	40		14	38·72		25	58·72		35	25·00	9	26·28	− 0·02
	48	50		14	49·70		25	58·70		35	25·03	9	26·33	+ 0·03
	49	0		14	58·76		25	58·76		35	25·06	9	26·30	0·00
	49	20		15	18·88		25	58·88		35	25·11	9	26·23	− 0·07
	49	30		15	29·84		25	58·84		35	25·14	9	26·30	0·00
	49	40		15	39·86		25	59·86		35	25·17	9	26·31	+ 0·01
	49	50		15	49·90		25	59·90		35	25·19	9	26·29	− 0·01
	50	0		15	58·90		25	58·90		35	25·22	9	26·32	+ 0·02
13	12	0		38	2·70		26	2·70		35	28·92	9	26·22	− 0·08
	12	10		38	12·64		26	2·64		35	28·94	9	26·30	0·00
	12	20		38	22·64		26	2·64		35	28·97	9	26·33	+ 0·03
	12	30		38	32·70		26	2·70		35	29·00	9	26·30	0·00
	12	40		38	42·76		26	2·76		35	29·03	9	26·27	− 0·03
	12	50		38	52·80		26	2·80		35	29·06	9	26·26	− 0·04
13	13	0	17	39	2·76	4	26	2·76	4	35	29·08	9	26·32	+ 0·02

Telegraphic Signals from Madras to Roorkee, 1875, May 31.

Madras Signals.			Roorkee Records.			Difference. Roor.—Mad.			Relative Correction.			Roorkee West.		Residual Errors.
h.	m.	s.	h.	m.	s.	h.	m.	s.	h.	m.	s.	m.	s.	s.
13	13	10	17	39	12·82	4	26	2·82	4	35	29·11	9	26·29	— 0·01
	13	20		39	22·86 ·		26	2·86		35	29·14	9	26·28	— 0·02
	13	30		39	32·90		26	2·90		35	29·17	9	26·27	— 0·08
	13	40		39	42·05		26	2·95		35	29·20	9	26·25	— 0·05
	13	50		39	52·87		26	2·87		35	29·22	9	26·35	+ 0·05
	14	0		40	2·04		26	2·94		35	29·25	9	26·31	+ 0·01
	14	10		40	12·98		26	2·98		35	29·28	9	26·30	0·00
	14	20		40	23·02		26	3·02		35	29·31	9	26·29	— 0·01
	14	.30		40	33.01		26	3·01		35	29·34	9	26·33	+ 0·03
	14	40		40	43.06		26	3·06		35	29·36	9	26·30	0·00
	14	50		40	53·09		26	3·09		35	29·39	9	26·30	0·00
13	15	0	17	41	3.07	4	26	3·07	4	35	29·42	9	26·35	+ 0·05
13	1	19·19	17	27	20·01	4	26	0·82	4	35	27·12	9	26·30	0·028

Telegraphic Signals from Roorkee to Madras, 1875, May 31.

Madras Records.			Roorkee Signals.			Difference. Roor.—Mad.			Relative Correction.			Roorkee West.		Residual Errors.
h.	m.	s.	h.	m.	s.	h.	m.	s.	h.	m.	s.	m.	s.	s.
12	53	1·2	17	19	0	4	25	58·8	4	35	25·73	9	26·93	+ 0·01
	53	11·1		19	10		25	58·9		35	25·76	9	26·86	— 0·06
	53	21·2		19	20		25	58·8		35	25·79	9	26·90	+ 0·07
	53	31·4		19	30		25	58·6		35	25·81	9	27·21	+ 0·29
	53	41·4		19	40		25	58·6		35	25·84	9	27·24	+ 0·32
	53	51·1 ·		19	50		25	58·9		35	25·87	9	26·97	+ 0·05
	54	1·0		20	0		25	59·0		35	25·90	9	26·90	— 0·02
	54	11·0		20	10		25	59·0		35	25·93	9	26·93	+ 0·01
	54	21·0		20	20		25	59·0		35	25·95	9	26·95 ·	+ 0·03
	54	31·0		20	30		25	59·0		35	25·98	9	26·98	+ 0·06
	54	41·0		20	40		25	59·0		35	26·01	9	27·01	+ 0·09
	54	50·9		20	50		25	59·1		35	26·04	9	26·94	+ 0·02
	55	1·0		21	0		25	59·0		35	26·07	9	27·07	+ 0·15
	55	10·9		21	10		25	59·1		35	26·09	9	26·99	+ 0·07
12	55	20·9	17	21	20	4	25	59·1	4	35	26·12	9	27·02	+ 0·10

Telegraphic Signals from Roorkee to Madras, 1875, May 31. .

Madras Records.			Roorkee Siguals.			Difference. Roor.—Mad.			Relative Correction.			Roorkee West.		Rosidual Errors.
h.	m.	s.	h.	m.	s.	h.	m.	s.	h.	m.	s.	m.	s.	s.
12	55	31·0	17	21	30	4	25	59·0	4	35	26·15	9	27·15	+ 0·23
	55	40·8		21	40		25	59·2		35	26·18	9	26·98	+ 0·06
	55	50·7		21	50	·	25	50·3		35	26·20	9	26·90	– 0·02
	56	0·7		22	0		25	50·3		35	26·23	9	26·93	+ 0·01
13	17	57·0		44	0		26	3·0		35	29·91	9	26·91	– 0·01
	18	7·0		44	10		26	3·0		35	29·94	9	26·94	+ 0·02
	18	17·0		44	20		26	3·0		35	29·97	9	26·97	+ 0·05
	18	27·0		44	30		26	3·0		35	30·00	9	27·00	+ 0·08
	18	36·9		44	40		26	3·1		35	30·03	9	26·93	+ 0·01
	18	47·0		44	50		26	3·0		35	30·05	9	27·05	+ 0·13
	18	56·7		45	0		26	3·3		35	30·08	9	26·78	– 0·1𝟺·
	19	6·6		45	10		26	3·4		35	30·11	9	26·71	– 0·21
	19	16·6		45	20		26	3·4		35	30·14	9	26·74	– 0·18
	19	26·6		45	30		26	3·4		35	30·16	9	26·76	– 0·16
	19	36·5		45	40		26	3·5		35	30·19	9	26·69	– 0·23
	19	46·6		45	50		26	3·4		35	30·22	9	26·82	– 0·10
	19	56·5		46	0		26	3·5		35·	30·25	9	26·75	– 0·17
	20	6·6		46	10		26	3·4		35	30·28	9	26·88	– 0·04
·	20	16·5		46	20		26	3·5		35	30·30	9	26·80	– 0·12
	20	26·5		46	30		26	3·5		35	30·33	9	26·83	– 0·09
	20	46·4		46	50		26	3·6		35	30·39	9	26·79	– 0·13
13	20	56·4	17	47	0	4	26	3·6	4	35	30·42	9	26·82	– 0·10
13	6	36·75	17	32	37·84	4	26	1·09	4	35	28·01	9	26·92	0·098

Madras and Roorkee Time Corrections, 1875, June 2.

At .12h. 10m. by Shepherd's Electrical Clock, it was 0·76 second fast of Madras Mean Time, with an adopted daily rate of 0·68 second losing.

At 15h. 39m. by Lieut. Col. Tennant's Transit Clock, it was 3·87 seconds slow of Roorkee Sidereal Time, with an adopted daily rate of 0·60 second losing.

Hence at 12h. 19m. by Shepherd's Electrical Clock, the Relative Correction was 4h. 43m. 15·55s. and its change + 0·16433 second per minute.

Telegraphic Signals from Roorkee to Madras 1875, June 2.

Madras Records.			Roorkee Signals.			Difference. Roor.—Mad.			Relative Correction.			Roorkee West.		Residual Errors.
h.	m.	s.	h.	m.	s.	h.	m.	s.	h.	m.	s.	m.	s.	s.
12	13	12·1	16	47	0	4	33	47·9	4	43	14·60	9	26·70	0·00
	13	22·2		47	10		33	47·8		43	14·62	9	26·82	+ 0·12
	13	32·0		47	20		33	48·0		43	14·65	9	26·65	− 0·05
	13	42·1		47	30		33	47·9		43	14·68	9	26·78	+ 0·08
	13	52·2		47	40		33	47·8		43	14·71	9	26·91	+ 0·21
	14	2·1		47	50		33	47·9		43	14·73	9	26·83	+ 0·13
	14	12·0		48	0		33	48·0		43	14·76	9	26·76	+ 0·06
	14	22·0		48	10		33	48·0		43	14·79	9	26·79	+ 0·09
	14	32·0		48	20		33	48·0		43	14·82	9	26·82	+ 0·12
	14	42·0		48	30		33	48·0		43	14·84	9	26·84	+ 0·14
	14	52·0		48	40		33	48·0		43	14·87	9	26·87	+ 0·17
	15	1·9		48	50		33	48·1		43	14·90	9	26·80	+ 0·10
	15	12·0		49	0		33	48·0		43	14·93	9	26·93	+ 0·23
	15	21·7		49	10		33	49·3		43	14·95	9	26·65	− 0·05
	15	31·6		49	20		33	46·4		43	14·98	9	26·58	− 0·12
	15	41·5		49	30		33	48·5		43	15·01	9	26·51	− 0·19
	15	51·6		49	40		33	48·4		43	15·03	9	26·63	− 0·07
	16	1·6		49	50		33	48·4		43	15·06	9	26·66	− 0·04
	16	11·5		50	0		33	48·5		43	15·09	9	26·59	− 0·11
	43	7·2	17	17	0		33	52·8		43	19·51	9	26·71	+ 0·01
	43	17·1		17	10		33	52·9		43	19·54	9	26·64	− 0·06
	43	27·0		17	20		33	53·0		43	19·57	9	26·57	− 0·13
	43	37·0		17	30		33	53·0		43	19·59	9	26·59	− 0·11
	43	47·0		17	40		33	53·0		43	19·62	9	26·62	− 0·08
12	43	57·0	17	17	50	4	33	53·0	4	43	19·65	9	26·65	− 0·05

Telegraphic Signals from Roorkee to Madras, 1875, June 2.

Madras Records.			Roorkee Signals.			Difference. Roor.—Mad.			Relative Correction.			Roorkee West.			Residual Errors.
h.	*m.*	*s.*	*h.*	*m.*	*s.*	*h.*	*m.*	*s.*	*h.*	*m.*	*s.*	*m.*	*s.*		*s.*
12	44	7·0	17	18	0	4	33	53·0	4	43	19·68	9	26·66		− 0·02
	44	17·0		18	10		33	53·0		43	19·70	9	26·70		0·00
	44	27·0		18	20		33	53·0		43	19·73	9	26·73		+ 0·03
	44	37·0		18	30		33	53·0		43	19·76	9	26·76		+ 0·06
	44	47·0		18	40		33	53·0		43	19·79	9	26·79		+ 0·09
	44	56·8		19	50		33	53·2		43	19·81	9	26·61		− 0·09
	45	6·8		19	0		33	53·2		43	19·84	9	26·64		− 0·06
	45	16·8		19	10		33	53·2		43	19·87	9	26·67		− 0·03
	45	26·5		19	20		33	53·5		43	19·89	9	26·39		− 0·31
	45	36·6		19	30		33	53·4		43	19·92	9	26·52		− 0·18
	45	46·8		19	40		33	53·2		43	19·95	9	26·75		+ 0·05
	45	56·7		19	50		33	53·3		43	19·98	9	26·68		− 0·02
12	46	6·7	17	20	0	4	33	53·3	4	43	20·00	9	26·70		0·00
12	29	39·40	17	3	30·00	4	33	50·60	4	43	17·30	9	26·70		0·091

Telegraphic Signals from Madras to Roorkee, 1875, June 2.

Madras Signals.			Roorkee Records.			Difference. Roor.—Mad.			Relative Correction.			Roorkee West.			Residual Errors.
h.	*m.*	*s.*	*h.*	*m.*	*s.*	*h.*	*m.*	*s.*	*h.*	*m.*	*s.*	*m.*	*s.*		*s.*
12	20	10	16	53	59·56	4	33	49·56	4	43	15·74	9	26·18		0·00
	20	20		54	9·57		33	49·57		43	15·77	9	26·20		+ 0·02
	20	30		54	19·65		33	49·65		43	15·80	9	26·15		− 0·03
	20	40		54	29·57		33	49·57		43	15·82	9	26·25		+ 0·07
	20	50		54	39·60		33	49·60		43	15·85	9	26·25		+ 0·07
	21	0		54	49·66		33	49·66		43	15·88	9	26·22		+ 0·04
	21	10		54	59·68		33	49·68		43	15·91	9	26·23		+ 0·05
	21	20		55	9·75		33	49·76		43	15·93	9	26·17		− 0·01
	21	30		55	19·76		33	49·76		43	15·96	9	26·20		+ 0·02
	21	40		55	29·80		33	49·80		43	15·99	9	26·19		+ 0·01
	21	50		55	39·83		33	49·83		43	16·02	9	26·19		+ 0·01
	22	0		55	49·81		33	49·81		43	16·04	9	26·23		+ 0·05
	22	10		55	59·87		33	49·87		43	16·07	9	26·20		+ 0·02
	22	20		56	9·96		33	49·96		43	16·10	9	26·14		− 0·04
12	22	30	16	56	19·99	4	33	49·99	4	43	16·12	9	26·13		− 0·05

Telegraphic Signals from Madras to Roorkee, 1875, June 2.

Madras Signals.			Roorkee Records.			Difference. Roor.—Mad.			Relative Correction.			Roorkee West.		Residual Errors.
h.	m.	s.	h.	m.	s.	h.	m.	s.	h.	m.	s.	m.	s.	s.
12	22	40	16	56	29·96	4	33	49·96	4	43	16·15	9	26·19	+ 0·01
	22	50		56	39·95		33	49·95		43	16·18	9	26·23	+ 0·05
	23	0		56	50·04		33	50·04		43	16·21	9	26·17	− 0·01
	52	0	17	25	54·78		33	54·78		43	20·97	9	26·19	+ 0·01
	52	10		26	4·78		33	54·78		43	21·00	9	26·22	+ 0·04
	52	20		26	14·93		33	54·93		43	21·03	9	26·10	− 0·08
	52	30		26	24·94		33	54·94		43	21·05	9	26·11	− 0·07
	52	40		26	34·96		33	54·96		43	21·08	9	26·12	− 0·06
	52	50		26	44·96		33	54·96		43	21·11	9	26·15	− 0·03
	53	0		26	54·96		33	54·96		43	21·14	9	26·18	0·00
	53	10	27	5·00			33	55·00		43	21·16	9	26·16	− 0·02
	53	20		27	15·07		33	55·07		43	21·19	9	26·12	− 0·06
	53	30		27	25·06		33	55·06		43	21·22	9	26·16	− 0·02
	53	40		27	35·13		33	55·13		43	21·25	9	26·12	− 0·06
	53	50		27	45·08		33	55·08		43	21·27	9	26·19	+ 0·01
	54	0		27	55·10		33	55·10		43	21·30	9	26·20	+ 0·02
	54	10	28	5·11			33	55·11		43	21·33	9	26·22	+ 0·04
	54	20		28	15·28		33	55·28		43	21·36	9	26·08	− 0·10
	54	30		28	25·23		33	55·23		43	21·38	9	26·15	− 0·03
12	54	40	17	28	35·27	4	33	55·27	4	43	21·41	9	26·14	− 0·04
12	37	0·29	17	10	52·62	4	33	52·33	4	43	18·51	9	26·18	0·036

Madras and Roorkee Time Corrections, 1875, June 5.

At 11h. 34m. by Shepherd's Electrical Clock, it was 1·03 seconds fast of Madras Mean Time, with an adopted daily rate of 0·28 second gaining.

At 15h. 49m. by Lieut. Col. Tennant's Transit Clock, it was 5·18 seconds slow of Roorkee Sidereal Time, with an adopted daily rate of 1·00 second losing.

Hence at 11h. 51m. by Shepherd's Electrical Clock, the Relative Correction was 4h. 54m. 59·04s. and its change + 0·16339 second per minute.

Telegraphic Signals from Madras to Roorkee, 1875, June 5.

Madras Signals.			Roorkee Records.			Difference. Roor.—Mad.			Relative Correction.			Roorkee West.		Residual Errors.
h.	m.	s.	h.	m.	s.	h.	m.	s.	h.	m.	s.	m.	s.	s.
11	49	0	16	34	32·26	4	45	32·26	4	54	58·71	9	26·45	− 0·05
	49	10		34	42·36		45	32·36		54	58·74	9	26·38	− 0·12
	49	20		34	52·29		45	32·29		54	58·77	9	26·48	− 0·02
	49	30		35	2·33		45	32·33		54	58·79	9	26·46	− 0·04
	49	40		35	12·36		45	32·36		54	58·82	9	26·46	− 0·04
	49	50		35	22·37		45	32·37		54	58·85	9	26·48	− 0·02
	50	0		35	32·26		45	32·26		54	58·88	9	26·02	+ 0·12
	50	10		35	42·34		45	32·34		54	58·90	9	26·56	+ 0·06
	50	20		35	52·48		45	32·48		54	58·93	9	26·45	− 0·05
	50	30		36	2·59		45	32·59		54	58·96	9	26·37	− 0·13
	50	40		36	12·51		45	32·51		54	58·99	9	26·48	− 0·02
	50	50		36	22·54		45	32·54		54	59·01	9	26·47	− 0·03
	51	0		36	32·57		45	32·57		54	59·04	9	26·47	− 0·03
	51	10		36	42·59		45	32·59		54	59·07	9	26·48	− 0·02
	51	20		36	52·58		45	32·58		54	59·09	9	26·51	+ 0·01
	51	30		37	2·63		45	32·63		54	59·12	9	26·49	− 0·01
	51	40		37	12·64		45	32·64		54	59·15	9	26·51	+ 0·01
	51	50		37	22·63		45	32·63		54	59·18	9	26·55	+ 0·05
	52	0		37	32·70		45	32·70		54	59·20	9	26·50	0·00
12	1	0		46	34·16		45	34·16		55	0·67	9	26·51	+ 0·01
	1	10		46	44·17		45	34·17		55	0·70	9	26·53	+ 0·03
	1	20		46	54·23		45	34·23		55	0·73	9	26·50	0·00
	1	30		47	4·27		45	34·27		55	0·76	9	26·49	− 0·01
	1	40		47	14·30		45	34·30		55	0·78	9	26·48	− 0·02
12	1	50	16	47	24·32	4	45	34·32	4	55	0·81	9	26·49	− 0·01

Telegraphic Signals from Madras to Roorkee, 1875, *June* 5.

Madras Signals.			Roorkee Records.			Difference. Roor.—Mad.			Relative Correction.			Roorkee West.		Residual Errors.
h.	m.	s.	h.	m.	s.	h.	m.	s.	h.	m.	s.	m.	s.	s.
12	2	0	16	47	34·30	4	45	34·30	4	55	0·84	9	26·54	+ 0·04
	2	10		47	44·38		45	34·38		55	0·86	9	26·48	− 0·02
	2	20		47	54·32		45	34·32		55	0·89	9	26·57	+ 0·07
	2	30		48	4·40		45	34·40		55	0·92	9	26·52	+ 0·02
	2	40		48	14·46		45	34·46		55	0·95	9	26·49	− 0·01
	2	50		48	24·58		45	34·58		55	0·97	9	26·39	− 0·11
	3	0		48	34·46		45	34·46		55	1·00	9	26·54	+ 0·04
	3	10		48	44·47		45	34·47		55	1·03	9	26·56	+ 0·06
	3	20		48	54·54		45	34·54		55	1·05	9	26·51	+ 0·01
	3	30		49	4·56		45	34·56		55	1·08	9	26·52	+ 0·02
	3	40		49	14·64		45	34·64		55	1·11	9	26·47	− 0·03
	3	50		49	24·69		45	34·69		55	1·14	9	26·45	− 0·05
12	4	0	16	49	34·58	4	45	34·58	4	55	1·16	9	26·58	+ 0·08
11	56	30·00	16	42	3·44	4	45	33·44	4	54	59·94	9	26·50	0·039

Telegraphic Signals from Roorkee to Madras, 1875, *June* 5.

Madras Records.			Roorkee Signals.			Difference. Roor.—Mad.			Relative Correction.			Roorkee West.		Residual Errors.
h.	m.	s.	h.	m.	s.	h.	m.	s.	h.	m.	s.	m.	s.	s.
11	55	27·0	16	41	0	4	45	33·0	4	54	59·77	9	26·77	− 0·12
	55	37·2		41	10		45	32·8		54	59·79	9	26·99	0·00
	55	47·1		41	20		45	32·9		54	59·82	9	26·92	− 0·07
	55	57·1		41	30		45	32·9		54	59·85	9	26·95	− 0·04
	56	7·0		41	40		45	33·0		54	59·88	9	26·88	− 0·11
	56	17·0		41	50		45	33·0		54	59·90	9	26·90	− 0·09
	56	27·1		42	0		45	32·9		54	59·93	9	27·03	+ 0·04
	56	37·0		42	10		45	33·0		54	59·96	9	26·96	− 0·03
	56	47·0		42	20		45	33·0		54	59·98	9	26·98	− 0·01
	56	57·0		42	30		45	33·0		55	0·01	9	27·01	+ 0·02
	57	7·0		42	40		45	33·0		55	0·04	9	27·04	+ 0·05
	57	17·0		42	50		45	33·0		55	0·07	9	27·07	+ 0·08
	57	26·9		43	0		45	33·1		55	0·09	9	26·99	0·00
	57	37·0		43	10		45	33·0		55	0·12	9	27·12	+ 0·13
11	57	47·0	16	43	20	4	45	33·0	4	55	0·15	9	27·15	+ 0·16

Telegraphic Signals from Roorkee to Madras, 1875, June 5.

Madras Records.	Roorkee Signals.	Difference. Roor.—Mad.	Relative Correction.	Roorkee West.	Residual Errors.
h. m. s.	h. m. s.	h. m. s.	h. m. s.	m. s.	s.
11 57 57·0	16 43 30	4 45 33·0	4 55 0·17	9 27·17	+ 0·18
58 6·8	43 40	45 33·2	55 0·20	9 27·00	+ 0·01
58 16·6	43 50	45 33·4	55 0·23	9 26·83	− 0·16
58 26·8	44 0	45 33·2	55 0·26	9 27·06	+ 0·07
12 ·15 24·0	17 1 0	45 36·0	55 3·03	9 27·03	+ 0·04
15 34·0	1 10	45 36·0	55 3·05	9 27·05	+ 0·06
15 44·0	1 20	45 36·0	55 3·08	9 27·08	+ 0·09
15 54·0	1 30	45 36·0	55 3·11	9 27·11	+ 0·12
16 4·0	1 40	45 36·0	55 3·13	9 27·13	+ 0·14
16 13·9	1 50	45 36·1	55 3·16	9 27·06	+ 0·07
16 23·9	2 0	45 36·1	55 3·19	9 27·09	+ 0·10
16 33·9	2 10	45 36·1	55 3·22	9 27·12	+ 0·13
16 43·9	2 20	45 36·1	55 3·24	9 27·14	+ 0·15
16 53·8	2 30	45 36·2	55 3·27	9 27·07	+ 0·08
17 3·6	2 40	45 36·4	55 3·30	9 26·90	− 0·09
17 13·5	2 50	45 36·5	55 3·32	9 26·82	− 0·17
17 23·5	3 0	45 36·5	55 3·35	9 26·85	− 0·14
17 33·5	3 10	45 36·5	55 3·38	9 26·88	− 0·11
17 43·4	3 20	45 36·6	55 3·41	9 26·81	− 0·18
17 53·6	3 30	45 36·4	55 3·43	9 27·03	+ 0·04
18 3·4	3 40	45 36·6	55 3·46	9 26·86	− 0·13
18 13·3	3 50	45 36·7	55 3·49	9 26·79	− 0·20
12 18 23·4	17 4 0	4 45 36·6	4 55 3·51	9 26·91	− 0·08
12 6 55·35	16 52 30·00	4 45 34·65	4 55 1·64	9 26·99	0·092

Summary of Telegraphic Results. (Campbell and Tennant.)

1875.	Number of Signals.	Roorkee West.	Probable Error.	Compound Retardation.
		m. s.	s.	s.
May 31 ...	By 18 from Madras ...	9 26·31	± 0·007	0·340
„ „ ...	By 19 from Roorkee ...	9 26·99	± 0·017	
June 2 ...	By 18 from Roorkee ...	9 26·78	± 0·019	0·290
„ „	By 18 from Madras	9 26·20	± 0·006	
Mean	By 73 Signals	9 26·57	± 0·022	0·315

Summary of Telegraphic Results. (Chronographic Records.)

1875.	Number of Signals.	Roorkee West.	Probable Errors.	Compound Retardation.
		m. s.	s.	s.
May 31 ...	By 19 from Madras ...	9 26·30	± 0·005	0·335
,, ,, ...	By 18 from Roorkee ...	9 26·97	± 0·009	
June 2 ...	By 19 from Roorkee ...	9 26·78	± 0·008	0·315
,, ,, ...	By 17 from Madras ...	9 26·15	± 0·009	
,, 5 ...	By 19 from Madras ...	9 26·51	± 0·007	0·330
,, ,, ...	By 19 from Roorkee	9 27·17	± 0·008	
Mean	By 111 Signals	9 26·65	± 0·019	0·327

Adopted Telegraphic Results. (Pogson and Tennant.)

1875.	Number of Signals.	Roorkee West.	Probable Errors.	Compound Retardation.
		m. s.	s.	s.
May 31 ...	By 37 from Madras ...	9 26·30	± 0·004	0·310
,, ,, ...	By 37 from Roorkee ...	9 26·92	± 0·014	
June 2 ...	By 35 from Madras ...	9 26·18	± 0·005	0 260
,, ,, ...	By 38 from Roorkee ...	9 26·70	± 0·013	
,, 5 ...	By 38 from Madras ...	9 26·50	. ± 0·005	0·245
,, ,, ...	By 38 from Roorkee	9 26·99	± 0·013	

Final Results.

	h.	m.	s.
Madras Observatory East of Greenwich....	5	20	59·40
Roorkee West of Madras.		9	26·60
Roorkee East of Greenwich.	5	11	32·80
Probable Error of Signals and Madras Transits			± 0·020
Compound Retardation. (Current and Instruments.) ...			0·272

Summary of Final Results.

Place.	Station.	East Longitude.			Prob. Error.
		h.	m.	s.	s.
Karachi ...	Observatory of the G. T. Survey.	(4	27	52·95 ?)	± 0·024
Avanashi ...	N. R. Pogson's Transit Pillar ...	5	9	20·35	± 0·113
Roorkee ...	Lt.-Col. Tennant's Transit Pillar.	5	11	32·80	± 0·020
Pondicherry ..	Light House ...	5	19	20·69	± 0·020
Colombo ...	Government Flagstaff ...	5	19	21·96	± 0·021
Jaffna ...	Captain Tupman's Transit Pillar.	5	20	2·00	± 0·020
Muddapur ...	Professor Tacchini's Transit Pillar	5	46	21·48	± 0·018
Singapore ...	Government Flagstaff ...	6	55	22·96	± 0·020

Concluding Remarks.

Probable Errors.—It is much to be regretted that for Karachi, Roorkee, Muddapur and Singapore, no details of the local time determinations were furnished me by the observers at those stations. In the cases of Colombo and Jaffna also, although the most complete details were supplied to me by Captain Tupman; his solar altitudes being grouped, instead of separately worked out, prevented me from deducing the probable errors of his local time corrections, without making fresh calculations which I did not care to undertake. The consequence of these omissions is, that the probable errors for these six places show the uncertainty due to the Madras Time determinations and the telegraphic signals only; about 0·02 of a second and nearly the same in each case. The relative personal equations of the observers being unknown, except in one instance, *viz.*, Avanashi, the final probable errors given are no guide to the actual certainty of the results, but serve merely to indicate the approximate precision attainable, had the proper and necessary precautions of comparing the habits of observation, or better still of interchanging the observers, been possible. Some trifling mistakes were inadvertently made in combining the probable errors of the time determinations with those of the telegraphic signals; amounting to 0·014 second in the case of Jaffna; 0·006 in Karachi and Singapore, and 0·001 in Avanashi and Colombo.

2. *Preservation of Stations.*—At four of the stations the temporary pillar used for the Transit or other instrument employed is the sole reference for the longitude deduced. It is to be hoped that these will be carefully preserved, as otherwise, all the labor and expense incurred in the determinations will be lost.

3. *Karachi.*—The longitude of the Great Trigonometrical Survey Station at Karachi, as determined by Lieut.-Col. Campbell and Major Heaviside with their incomparably superior arrangements, carried from Madras through Bellary and Bombay to Karachi, give the latter station 4*h*. 28*m*. 3·62*s*. East of Greenwich. An error of exactly ten seconds in General Addison's time determination is the only possible explanation of this most unexpected difference; and supposing such to have been made, it would have a precisely reverse effect upon his determinations of the difference of longitude between Karachi and Ispahan, and would therefore be eliminated in the final difference between Greenwich and Madras, referred to on page 47. When communicating his longitude results to the Royal Astronomical Society (*Monthly Notices Vol. XXXVIII page* 83) General Addison remarked as follows :—" That for Karachi, has an element " of doubt in it, inasmuch as I neglected to obtain the pivot error of my " Transit Instrument. But to whatever extent the pivot error affected the " result as regards Karachi, the difference between Ispahan and Madras " remains unaffected, the errors on the East and West sides of Karachi " correcting each other."

No conceivable "*pivot correction,*" nor any other kind of instrumental error could account for so large a difference as exactly ten seconds of time ; so it seems pretty certain that the clock corrections furnished by General Addison should have been 19·50 seconds instead of 9·50 seconds, as adopted on page 49, for finding the relative correction of the signals. This would give the following numbers to be substituted for those in the "*Final Results,*" on pages 54 and 80 ; bringing our value of the longitude within 0·67 second of that found by the Officers of the G. T. Survey.

	h.	*m.*	*s.*
General Addison's Station West of Madras ...	0	52	55·85
G. T. Survey Observatory East of Greenwich ...	4	28	2·95

4. *Roorkee*—The longitude of this station, deduced trigonometrically, was kindly communicated to me by General J. T. Walker R. E., then Surveyor General of India, in November ·1880, as 5*h*. 11*m*. 33·23*s*., which is 0·43 second greater than the telegraphic determination.

Colonel Tennant, in his "*Report on the Transit of Venus*," page 5, remarks, for reasons there stated ;—" The geodesical position of Roorkee, therefore, is not likely to agree with the astronomical determination."

5. *Pondicherry.*—General J. T. Walker at the same time favored me with the trigonometrically determined difference of longitude between Madras and Pondicherry. Applied to the now adopted longitude of Madras, this gives Pondicherry, 5*h*. 19*m*. 20·66*s*. East of Greenwich ; which is only 0·03 second less ·than was found by Messrs. Fleuriais and myself in 1870.

6. *Colombo and Jaffna.*—A valuable check upon these determinations was afforded by a direct telegraphic comparison between Captain Tupman at Jaffna and Captain Donnan at Colombo. Their difference was 39·36 seconds, while that resulting from the independent determination of each station with Madras was 40·04 seconds ; as close as could be reasonably expected from solar altitude time determinations and three unknown personal equations involved in the operations.

7. *Singapore.*—It has already been mentioned, on page 12, that the result of the American Expedition in January 1882 shewed an excess of 0·54 second over that found by Prof. Oudemans and myself in 1871. The agreement is however sufficiently satisfactory for all present requirements.

In scientific undertakings dependent upon an individual, perfect freedom from all restraint is most calculated to secure the best attainable results ; but when co-operation is necessary a programme is indispensable, and can neither be too definitely laid down and studied beforehand, nor too rigidly adhered to in its execution.

www.ingramcontent.com/pod-product-compliance
Lightning Source LLC
Chambersburg PA
CBHW032349020726
47499CB00008B/2685